The Touchstone of Raven Hollow

Secrets of Roseville • Book 3

Betty Bolté

This is a work of fiction. Names, characters, places, and incidents are a product of the author's imagination. Locales and public names are sometimes used for atmospheric purposes. Any resemblance to actual people, living or dead, or to businesses, companies, events, institutions, or locales is completely coincidental.

Betty Bolté
www.bettybolte.com

To Crystal,
for all her guidance and inspiration.

Chapter One

"Damn. I can't do this."

If pride caused one to fall, she had nothing to fear. She took no pride in her cooking nor her gift. Everything she tried turned out either mediocre or a dismal failure. She hid any hint of talent or ability. She preferred to get through her life without anyone unmasking her for who and what she was. And yet today loomed ahead as yet another opportunity for proving she couldn't meet the expectations set before her.

Tara Golden stared out the kitchen door, frowning at the familiar scene for several frantic beats of her heart. Morning sunshine filtered through the waxy leaves of a tall magnolia, illuminating the covered fire pit and surrounding rustic chairs nestled in the far reaches of the yard. The conversation corner in the backyard had witnessed many evenings of laughter and shared secrets. Quiet and private, she escaped to her favorite chair as often as possible. Perhaps she'd snatch a book and brave the November chill. Forget about the pressure to succeed, to pass the unspoken and unfair test, yet again filling her gut with trepidation. No matter how hard she tried.

She pressed her fingers to both temples, trying to quiet

her mind as well as her rapid pulse. Her sisters hadn't emerged from their rooms yet, so she had a little time to indulge her whim. She turned away from the window, already mentally sifting through the titles on the shelf at the other end of the room. Just a few minutes would alleviate some of the stress in her soul. As she walked away from the door, her gaze landed on the empty bakery box on the countertop. She dropped her hands, fingers curling into fists, pushing against her legs.

"Double damn." She'd forgotten the buns warming in the oven. She inhaled as she brushed her hair away from her face, pulling it up into a ponytail that grazed her shoulders.

The sweet smell of hot cinnamon and sugar filled the kitchen with memories. Memories of her mother cooking and baking up a storm for family meals. Before she'd died so suddenly three years before. A tear fell on Tara's cheek, and she rubbed the moisture away. She'd cried enough. She surveyed the cozy room, aware of the lingering sense of intruding into a special place ricocheting in her heart. Almost as if she sensed her mother's presence. She hoped not. Although she missed her mother desperately, it helped to think that her mom had found peace. Perhaps one day Tara might also find inner peace. If she ever managed to tame the guilt monster who clawed inside every time she thought of how her mother died.

"Something smells yummy." Beth strode into the sunny room and headed straight for the coffee pot. She wore a forest green pullover sweater with cream corduroy jeans, emphasizing her slim figure. Bunny slippers with floppy ears completed the outfit with a bit of whimsy. Cup in hand, Tara's older sister pivoted to peer at her. Her expression indicated she'd detected the hot sweet aroma. "Do I smell sticky buns?"

"Yeppers." Tara waved a hand toward the oven as she

moved to stand by the center island. She braced a hand on the edge of the counter, noting Beth appeared pulled together as always. "They're best warm."

Tara had chosen khaki jeans, a black cable knit sweater, and black loafers, ready to head to the Golden Owl Books and Brews store right after she finished breakfast. A utilitarian uniform. Ugh. Compared to the trim outfit her next older sister wore, she probably looked dowdy at best. She didn't want to think about how others viewed her attire. She never seemed able to live up to expectations. Her own or her sisters.

"As if you made them yourself, right?" Beth chuckled and then sipped from the steaming mug. "You're not fooling anyone; you know that right?"

She knew it. Tara relived the memories of her mother, Peggy Golden, most every day. Recalled how smart, pretty, and competent she'd been. Envisioning her bustling about the small yet efficient kitchen, an apron covering her slacks and top, while she stirred or sautéed or whatever task necessary to make the most amazing meals. Repasts good for both body and soul. The elegant cakes and tarts, pies and puddings, also caused people to exclaim over them. Tara's kitchen magic was weak by comparison. Despite her best efforts, her meals ended up workmanlike and plain, much like her choice of attire, even if they did nourish the body. The soul was left to fend for itself.

"I'm not trying to." Tara shrugged off her sister's observation. Everyone knew she was not the baker of the family. Sure, she baked occasionally, but never anything fancy or difficult. She couldn't compete with her sisters in the kitchen. Roxie, in particular, seemed capable of accomplishing anything she set out to do. Tara was not so fortunate. But ask her to make a salad, and she'd whip up the best combination of healthy vegetables and lean protein with a delicious, low-fat dressing any day. She preferred simple and easy to elaborate and difficult. "See? There's the box from the bakery in plain view for all to see."

Beth leaned forward to peruse the label, her golden locks falling around her cheeks to hang over the counter. "The new one over on Poplar Street?"

"The Sweet Serendipity has a nice variety of breakfast buns and bagels." She'd been tempted to buy more than she had but decided to limit the indulgence. Her thighs thanked her. "I imagine I'll be a regular customer."

"Where?" Roxie strolled in, pushing up the sleeves of her crimson Alabama sweatshirt to just below her elbows. Faded blue jeans and brown loafers completed her outfit. Sensible and neat described her perfectly. Roxie spotted the white paperboard box sitting open on the counter and nodded, making her brown and gold ponytail swing side to side. "I see."

"Tara..." Beth pointed toward the stove with a manicured finger. "I think you need to take them out."

"No, they need a few more minutes to be good and gooey warm." Tara pivoted to reassure herself after the note of warning in Beth's voice. "Oh!"

She raced to open the door only to cough as smoke poured into the room, triggering the smoke alarm on the ceiling to blare her embarrassment for all their neighbors to hear. She grabbed the hot pads and quickly pulled the flimsy aluminum pan from the hot interior, popping and smoking, and plopped it on top of the range. With a flick of her wrist, she snapped the dial to the left to turn off the heat. Spinning around, she covered her ears to dampen the blaring of the obnoxious alarm. Beth had opened the outside door while Roxie used the bakery box to fan the smoke away from the noise maker. After several minutes, the shrieking stopped and Tara forced her shoulders into their normal position. What had she expected?

"You used to know your way around the kitchen, Tara."

Roxie tossed the box onto the counter and then retrieved a mug from the rack by the coffee maker. Pouring the dark liquid into the cup, she glanced at Tara. "You need to get over it."

"I'm not sure I can." Tara wouldn't even pretend not to catch her sister's allusion so casually tossed in her direction.

She'd been busy in the kitchen the day her mother died. Baking a lemon cake for her birthday as a surprise. Decorating the layers with chocolate frosting and then writing in yellow buttercream icing had taken forever but she'd managed to finish it with time to spare. Pride had swelled her chest for a change. Not only had she managed to make the two layers the same size without sloping one direction or the other. The writing even ended up legible. Her mother would have been very pleased with how neatly she'd written with the recalcitrant icing.

Only the surprise had been on Tara when she had gone into her mother's bedroom where she'd gone for a nap. She'd felt tired and had a slight ache in her jaw and head. Tara had offered to ease her discomfort, but her mother had insisted it wasn't necessary. A little rest and she'd be good as new. Tara eased up to the side of the bed, and whispered to her. No response, no shift, no eyes opening. Tara gently shook her mother's shoulder and then froze. Her mother had died in her sleep. Alone. Tara had so much she wanted to share with her mother. Then to never have the opportunity, or even the chance to say goodbye. Tears had flowed until she thought she'd choke on them. But arrangements had to be made and people informed of her passing. The following days remained a foggy blur of condolences and sadness. The whole town turned out for her mother's funeral. Since Peggy ran the only bookstore in the area around Roseville, Tennessee, everyone knew and adored her.

"It wasn't your fault. It wasn't anyone's." Roxie crossed

to Tara's side and peered at her. "You need to put all that behind you and move forward. It's what Mom would have wanted."

How could anyone know what their mother would have asked of them had she lived? People say that they know, but do they really? Peggy Golden had been the sun the three sisters revolved around. They had lived together in the historic home for as long as Tara could remember. Longer, since she was the youngest. She barely remembered her father, Roscoe Golden, as a big man with a big laugh. He'd died before she started kindergarten, leaving her mother to raise the three girls by herself. A cohesive unit until the sun burned out and left the planets to drift apart on their own. Somehow she had to find her way without the pull of a central force.

"They're not too black if you want one." Tara motioned to the pan of sticky buns and then refilled her coffee cup. She'd not apologize for knowing her limitations. An envelope Roxie apparently liked to push farther and farther. At some point, the barrier would break and then she'd fail resplendently. She didn't want to contemplate such a dismal event. "You're braver than I am to wear that to work."

"Do you think folks will mind here in Volunteer territory?" Roxie dipped her head to glance at the stylized white A on the front of the sweatshirt and then grinned at Tara. "I'm not wearing it to the store. I have some errands to run this morning so thought I'd risk it about town. You know, to get a reaction."

One thing the oldest sister could count on was eliciting a reaction from others. Her personality and her attitude seemed to poke and prod people into a strong retort. Always had. Both positive and negative responses seemed to come with an added measure of punch. As if the very air around Roxie intoxicated her audience, reducing their ability to suppress their emotions much like the effect of alcohol.

"I'm sure you will. This small town has a tendency to think small as well." Beth shook her head in mock disapproval, her long hair brushing her shoulders. She studied Roxie's attire for several moments. "You'll surely get noticed. For better or worse."

"That's what I'm hoping for." Roxie burst out laughing, her shoulders shaking as she slapped a hand over her mouth. She moved to the other side of the island, still chuckling. After she regained control, she winked at Beth. "I know I shouldn't do it. Some folks think it's mean. But I love to push buttons."

"You're good at it, too." Tara sipped her coffee before setting the cup on the counter. The sound of Roxie's laughter reminded Tara of her father's, a faint echo of memory decades old.

Beth's dig at the people of Roseville hinted at a growing dissatisfaction with small town life. Not that Beth had said as much, but the increase in the number of snarky observations sparked suspicions of her intent, whether she was aware of them or not. Tara cradled the mug in both hands as she shifted her attention to her oldest sister. She seemed different on this fall morning. The longer she contemplated Roxie, the more certain she became of a change in the air. Not just the clearing of the burned sugar smell, either. Better to find out up front than to leave the lingering sensation to tickle her conscious for hours or days. Been there, done that.

Tara cleared her throat, fingers wrapped around her cold cup. "Speaking of buttons being pushed, you look like you've got a surprise up your sleeve. What's with the grin?"

Roxie aimed hazel eyes at Tara and placed her hands on the island, leaning on the surface to support her torso. "You've always been able to read my moods. That's part of your gift. You're right. I do have a surprise. Can you guess?"

Her sisters accepted her special abilities because they possessed their own gifts. Ones they employed with extreme caution so others wouldn't suspect. Or at least that was her goal. Roxie tended to hide her proclivities in plain sight, her gift centered in the language of spells and incantations. Beth's gift also was easy to hide. Visions of the future could only be seen in her mind, after all. But Tara's proved impossible to hide completely. She'd tried over the years, but had only mastered subtlety as a smokescreen. Her talent lay in detecting the health and wellbeing of a person and then her touch would set matters aright. But first, she had to determine what was amiss. All of which could require the laying on of hands, literally, which could be tricky to do without raising questions.

She had first discovered her powers when a little girl. Playing at the school with her classmates. One classmate had climbed onto the jungle gym on a sunny, late August day despite the teacher warning the children away from the hot metal. Tara had gravitated toward her, sensing danger and a looming need. But nobody else reacted to the strange sight, the pulsating energy, so she kept mum. Waited with mounting fear for someone else to step in and stop the imminent accident. When the small hand wrapped around first one and then the next bar of the metal playground apparatus, Tara jerked in sympathy. After only a few swings from one to the next, the girl had screamed and dropped to the ground near where Tara watched in horror. The air between them vibrated and pulsed, shimmering and glowing in a terrifying way.

A compulsion overcame her paralysis at the sight of the crying girl and forced her to run to her side and grab both of her raw palms in her own. Tingling in Tara's fingers cooled her palms until the heat in the other girl's hands dissipated like fog before the sun. When she'd removed her hands, Tara was shocked to see the girl's palms healed as if never injured. The girl had looked at Tara with a grateful yet fearful expression and then jumped up and ran away to surround herself with her friends. Leaving Tara alone and scared with no one to turn to for an explanation of what had occurred.

The looks from her classmates warned Tara something weird and unexplained had happened. Something frightening to everyone around her, including herself. After school recessed for the day, she'd confided to her mother the events of the morning while sitting in the conversation corner. Away from eavesdropping or nosy neighbors. Away from the prying eyes of passersby. Her mother's revelations as to the sisters' true nature proved eye-opening. She'd learned very quickly to keep her ability hidden to avoid being ostracized by others.

As she'd grown older, she'd learned when and how to use her talents. She'd chosen to become an official healer in the form of a licensed midwife in order to provide cover for her healing touch. Brief touches over a short period proved as effective as a longer contact. When she was with her sisters, though, she could employ her gift. Together in their own house, they were safe.

Tara tilted her head to one side and studied her oldest sister for several moments. She sensed Roxie had made a decision, one involving her and Beth. "What have you settled on that we may not approve of?"

"Oh, you're good! I'm sure you'll never guess, so I'll have to tell you." Roxie put her hands on her hips, bracing to reveal her bombshell as a wide smile split her face. She tossed her head, her ponytail whipping over one shoulder. "Paulette called, and she mentioned Grant Markel arrived out at the plantation yesterday unannounced to share Thanksgiving with his brother and her since their parents elected to go on a world cruise over the holidays. She and Zak have tickets tonight for a dinner theater with Meredith and Max, and she was worried about Grant being left all alone."

Grant? Tara's heart raced at the thought of the handsome man she'd tried so hard to forget. She'd secretly helped him the month before when he'd accompanied Zak to town in search of some alchemical solution to his desperate medical condition. Several presses of her fingers to his temples were all she needed to save him. Then he'd gone home, and she'd strived to push him out of her mind. Away from her heart.

Yet how could she forget his dove gray eyes smiling at her as they danced? Or the way his thick brown hair with red and gold highlights caught the light from the disco ball on the ceiling? His muscular shoulders swaying to the beat of the energetic tune? The zing of electricity flowing through her fingers when she touched his temples? He was a gorgeous sight, but there was one huge problem. She had no intention of leaving Roseville, her home, or her sisters. When he'd returned to Michigan and his home and work after his week's visit, she had moved on. Well, tried to move forward.

Roxie lifted a charred but still gooey bun from the pan, picking off the black edges with pincer fingers. Taking a bite, she moaned with delight as she chewed and swallowed. At least the buns still tasted good. A plus in Tara's favor.

"He's such a hunk of man. I would love to get to know him better." Beth tapped a finger on the red-and-white checked tablecloth, leaning back in her chair, one brow quirked and lips slightly parted.

Beth's comment sparked a bolt of jealousy, one Tara quickly suppressed. Beth could have him if she wanted him. Tara shot a glance at Roxie, noting the laughter in her eyes as she finished her bun in several quick bites. When Roxie turned her gaze to Tara, her heart sank. "What have you done?"

"I told her we'd be happy to help keep him busy." Roxie cleaned her fingers on a paper napkin then tossed it into the trash. "He'll come over this evening for dinner."

"Tonight? It's taco night." Tara shook her head, her ponytail whipping her cheeks. Each sister took turns with the cooking so as to share the task or the fun, as the case may be. Today was Tara's day to handle the onerous chore. "I don't want to be responsible for making dinner for him. Let Beth do it instead."

"Why?" Roxie swiveled her head to frown at Tara. "It's the perfect night since he can pick and choose what he wants. It'll be fine."

"Come on, Tara, don't be a wimp." Beth pushed out her chair and stood, bracing one hand on a hip. "Tacos are the easiest thing to make. Even you can't mess them up."

"We'll see." Tara dragged in a breath and let it out with a huff. She'd never had a problem before, so perhaps her sister was right. "Fine. But don't blame me if it all goes wrong."

Roxie sidled over to hug Tara with one arm, her free hand resting on Tara's upper arm, giving her a brief squeeze. "Relax. We've got your back. Besides, it's just Grant, and he's family now."

"Extended family. Through marriage." Tara managed to squash the desire to roll her eyes at the idea of the brawny geologist as close family. "His brother, Zak, married our cousin, Paulette, so that makes Grant, what?"

"A cousin-in-law?" Beth chuckled as she lifted her keys from the hook and headed for the back door. "I've got to get to the bookstore. See you all later."

"I've got to run, too." Roxie dropped her arms to pivot on one foot, snatch her purse from the shelf by the key rack, and follow Beth through the door. The jingle of keys cut off when the door bumped closed.

Alone, Tara surveyed the mess in the kitchen and tossed

a quick prayer to the patron saints of cooking, whoever they may be, to give her guidance. Pushing up her sweater sleeves to the elbow, she picked up the blackened foil pan and tossed it into the garbage. Best to keep busy and not dwell on her shortcomings. The day had to get better. *Triple damn.* Had she just jinxed herself?

Chapter Two

$\mathcal{F}$oolish and yet determined. Grant mentally shook his head at his folly as he stared out the parlor window at the lake in front of the manor house. Nevertheless, he'd arrived at Twin Oaks plantation where his brother now lived with his new wife, Paulette, ready to discover the solution to the so-called miracle. Miracle, indeed. He didn't believe in inexplicable phenomena or the supernatural. His doctors apparently did, though, calling the unexplained cure of the tumors in his head miraculous. No way. Something about the town of Roseville or the Twin Oaks plantation held the explanation, the answer, a clue. He planned to discover it and then return home and set the record straight. The doctors would learn a lesson about believing in such nonsense as miracles and he would be able to pursue his new future. One that included more satisfying work than being an analyst in a testing lab as well as a wife and family of his own. Nearly losing his sight or dying had woken him up and set his feet on an entirely different path.

"I'm glad to see you, bro," Zak spoke from where he paused in the doorway and then sauntered into the double parlor and stopped beside the love seat. "If you'd let us know you were coming, we'd have gotten you a ticket."

"Our folks weren't going to be around." Grant shook his head as he turned to face his older brother. "It was a last-minute decision, so don't worry about it."

Zak's inky black hair shone in the chandelier lighting, his gray eyes crinkling at the corners as he flopped onto the small sofa. He fished a slip of paper out of his shirt pocket and handed it to Grant. "I'm not, especially since you'll be entertained this evening by the Golden sisters."

"Excuse me?" Grant glanced at the paper and noted a street address. He sank abruptly onto the chair opposite the love seat and stared at the smirk aimed his direction. His older brother loved to discomfit him. Not this time. "I thought I'd just hang out here, rest after the long drive yesterday. That sort of thing."

In fact, lounging around in the huge antebellum-era house sounded like a fine way to spend the evening. Pacing through the single and double parlors, the sewing room, the updated kitchen. Maybe even wander outside to the gazebo to read until the sun set and the air chilled. Then a bowl of bubbling chili topped with cheese and onions and a cold brew. He'd be all set.

He was tired and wanted nothing more than to rest and think through his next move. He'd spent the day retracing his steps from his visit before Halloween. He poked around the bedroom Meredith had put him in for the second time. The comfortable bed and cheerful furnishings held no clues or answers. He checked the water, using his portable testing kit, but no unusual elements were revealed. Simple well water. The pillow's composition seemed to be foam, so that couldn't have affected his illness. Sniffing, he had smelled nothing unexpected on a fall day in the country. What about the undetectable elements? He'd need an air sample tested. Somewhere, somehow he intended to find the truth and put an end to the ludicrous idea of a mystical cure for his tumors.

Zak shook his head with a big grin. "The ladies are looking forward to having you join them for dinner. Six o'clock, and don't be late."

"You didn't have to arrange for them to take care of me. I'm a big boy and can fend for myself." Grant rested his hands on his knees, contemplating Zak's expression. "I know how to open a can, after all."

Zak's chuckle echoed in the large room despite the carpet on the hardwood floor and the drapes at the windows. The snap and crackle of the fire in the firebox filled the brief silence. A welcoming space in the impressive house, one he had enjoyed during his previous visit. Knowing Twin Oaks had plenty of rooms to accommodate guests—Paulette and Meredith had run it as a B&B before their double wedding—he had made the abrupt decision to make the journey and stay with his brother until he'd located the source of his cure. His mission, not a vacation.

"I know, but it will do you good to get out and have some fun." Zak's smile faded into a hint of a grin. "You'll be surrounded by three gorgeous women all to yourself. If I weren't married…"

"What would you do?" Paulette strode into the room, a tray bearing plates of cookies and sliced apples in her hand. Wearing dark blue leggings and a flowered tunic, she appeared to have adapted to being a wife and mother with little change to her outward appearance. She quirked a brow at her husband and set the tray on the coffee table between the two men. "I'd like to know."

"Nothing, my beautiful, loving wife." Zak surged to his feet to seal his statement with a kiss on Paulette's neck. "I'm married, so it doesn't matter, right?"

"Good answer." She kissed him back and then broke away to address Grant. "Would you care for some tea or a cocktail while we wait for Meredith and Max to get ready?"

"I'm driving into town later, so I'll take a beer." At least he'd get the brew part of his fantasy. "Just one though."

"I'll be right back." Paulette started to pivot and then speared Zak with a look. "Behave yourself." Then she sashayed out of the room and turned toward the kitchen.

Zak let out a burst of laughter and sank onto the love seat. "Enjoy being around the sisters. They're full of surprises."

"If you're talking about their Halloween costumes which became bridesmaid's dresses, then I know what you mean." Grant rubbed his thighs, the rasp of his hands on his jeans a soft disturbance in the quiet parlor. "Imagine dressing as witches for your wedding. The poor minister. I thought he'd collapse at the very idea."

Memories floated in his mind of the array of costumes for the party that morphed into a wedding a few days later. After a purported ghost had abruptly but unlikely ended the party. And Paulette just as abruptly had her baby. When the baby's absentee father suddenly showed up, tensions ran high until Zak convinced the jerk to leave mother and child in peace. Followed by the double wedding. A busy few days to say the least. Grant was glad he'd been there to stand as Zak's best man, but the whole scene had been unnerving. They all seemed to believe in witches and ghosts. A thought that made him shake his head at the absurdity. But who was he to tell them what to believe in?

Zak chuckled and reached for a chocolate chip cookie, popping it whole into his mouth and chewing as he eyed Grant. "I'll never forget my anniversary, that's for sure."

"Good point." Grant shook his head as he tapped a hand on one knee. "Paulette may not take it kindly if you did."

"Likely. So, bro, you're going to see Tara this evening." Zak shot a smirk at Grant as he reached for another cookie. "Paulette tells me she studiously avoids mentioning your name."

Interesting observation. Tara had enthralled him at the party, the way she flirted with him and made him feel as if he existed in the center of her world. If only for a few brief hours. Before he'd been forced to return to his world. The big city suited his temperament with its thriving populace and energy. Or at least it always had, until his health crisis opened his eyes to what was important. To what he'd shunted to one side but now proved all-consuming. "Why would she have a reason to talk about me?"

"No reason." Zak regarded him for a beat, leaning against the love seat again. "Except for the fact that you're my brother and I do have occasion to mention you and the work you're doing."

"Boring them, I'm sure." Or was it? Could Tara possibly have any interest in his work? That would be something unique in his experience.

"Imagine how bored they become when I talk about chemical engineering." Zak folded his hands over one knee as he regarded Grant. "At least they don't doze off."

Previous women Zak had dated had literally fallen asleep at the table before he'd learned to stick to lighter fare. Music. Movies. Books. Grant had benefitted from his older brother's experience as far as knowing what topics to discuss with the girls he'd taken out while in high school. Somehow he didn't believe they'd care for a lengthy chat about the composition of various kinds of rocks. Or the contents of the layers of sedimentary rocks. Or how fissures are related to earthquakes. So he made sure to be informed about art, movies, books, and other cultural subjects.

"About tonight." Grant rose and paced to the fireplace. Leaning an elbow on the mantel, he carefully avoided the grouping of framed photographs flanked by hurricane globes with gold pillar candles flickering inside. Pictures of Paulette's sister, Meredith, and her lawyer husband, Max, standing by the lake out front of the house. Of Zak and

Paulette laughing in an immense pile of colorful leaves. Of Paulette holding their newborn son. No one could miss the love between the trio or doubt Zak's love for his new family. "Do you have a sitter?"

"Yes. Max arranged for his secretary to keep Pat overnight at her place. He's already safely ensconced in Sue's happy, grandmotherly arms."

"She's a good woman to take care of him." He recalled the feisty middle-aged lady with her vivacious manner that belied her age while she danced at the wedding reception. "I have one more question for you."

"What's that?" Zak bit into a slice of apple as Paulette strode into the parlor, a bottle of beer in one hand and a flowered mug in the other.

"Here you go." Paulette handed him the dark brown bottle and then sat beside Zak. She sipped from the mug of steaming tea, the mingled scents of honey and orange fighting with the smell of wood smoke. "Enjoy."

Grant nodded his thanks and then addressed his brother. "Where can I get a decent bottle of wine to take with me? I can't go empty handed."

Zak settled on the sofa and wrapped an arm around Paulette's shoulders. He thought for a moment. "There's a little shop next to the grocery store that carries a good selection and has good prices too."

"I think the girls are serving tacos tonight. It's Tara's night to cook, according to Roxie." Paulette looked at Zak and then up at Grant. "Maybe some Mexican beer would be a better fit?"

What did he know? Didn't women prefer wine? He'd enjoy a good Corona or Dos Equis. "Do the girls like beer?"

Zak angled his head as he turned to snare Paulette with his quizzical frown. "I've never seen them drink it…"

Paulette shrugged and sipped from the cup of tea. "Wine is a safe choice and would be fine with tacos."

"You think wine is fine with anything." Zak grinned at her, squeezing her shoulders.

"True." She lowered the mug to rest on her thigh. "I'd pick a Merlot, I think, to go with the spices in the meat."

The cold bottle sweated as he lifted it to take several swallows. Wiping his mouth with his free hand, he nodded. "Good idea. Although I didn't come here to have dinner with your cousins. I came here to—"

"I've been wondering why you showed up at our door without even letting us know you were heading this way." Paulette sipped, rested the mug on her leg, and then snuggled against Zak's side. "What's up?"

Seeing his brother content and happy with his new beautiful bride contrasted sharply with his own lonely life. A life that would have been much different if not for the end of the tumors threatening to steal his eyesight and thus his ability to perform his job as a geologist. He worked in the lab testing various samples and specimens for their composition. While boring, the analysis yielded results necessary for builders and others to choose the appropriate materials for their construction and other projects. Beyond just his chosen profession, though, the tumors had threatened his entire lifestyle. Everything would have changed, and not for the better, if the tumors had succeeded in their aim. Thank goodness he had retained his vision. But he must understand the cure to put to rest the claim of a miracle. Perhaps the real miracle arrived in the form of a change in his perspective and plans for his life.

"I'm in search of the reason for why the brain scans came back clean after I stayed here last month." He smoothed a hand over his jaw, noting the stubble. A quick glance at his watch confirmed he'd best excuse himself to shave and dress for the evening's entertainment. "The doctors said it's a miracle, but there must be an explanation.

Do you think it was something in that Elixir thing you were trying to make?"

Zak gaped at him for a long moment before slowly shaking his head. "I never finished making the Elixir of Life, so it couldn't have been that wild idea of mine."

"It was pretty far-fetched to think some alchemist held the answer." Grant swigged another swallow. "I need to know what cured me. Not just for my benefit, but for the others who suffer from the disease. Any ideas of where I should search?"

Paulette stared at him, mouth slightly open. She blinked several times without speaking. She glanced at Zak and then met Grant's gaze. What had he said to cause such a curious reaction? As though she withheld some important information from him. A frown settled on his brows as he pondered the surprise and consternation evident in her expression. She turned to look at her husband and then at her tea mug. Raising her gaze once more to meet his, she shrugged.

Zak cleared his throat to draw Grant's attention back to his placid countenance. "I hope you find the answer you're searching for. How long do you plan to stay?"

As long as it took. Or until Zak threw him out. "Through Thanksgiving, if that's okay?"

Another exchanged glance and then matching smiling faces regarded him. As if they shared a secret he wasn't privy to. What was up with them?

"Sounds good." Zak gave a last squeeze to Paulette's shoulder and then pushed to his feet. He held out a hand to her, palm up in invitation. "Shall we get ready for this evening?"

"Definitely." Paulette placed her hand in his and stood, setting her mug on the tray in one fluid motion. "I hope you enjoy yourself tonight, Grant. Those three sure know how to keep life interesting."

A hint of relief in her voice made him peer at her, inspecting her expression for some hidden meaning. Detecting nothing but a pleasant smile and steady gaze, he mentally shrugged away his suspicions.

"I'll try to enjoy being surrounded by beautiful women, though I'd prefer to not impose on them." Taking the last swig from the bottle, he placed it on the tray and wiped his damp hand on his jeans. "Then tomorrow I'll continue my search for answers in earnest."

Chapter Three

*E*dna's Grocery bustled with customers in the late afternoon, the parking lot a steady stream of cars and pickup trucks coming and going. Tara strolled along the sidewalk, pulling a small wagon rattling over the seams and cracks as she made her way to pick up the ingredients for dinner. Since most of what she needed was perishable, she didn't buy them until the day she would use them to have them at their freshest. Mulling the possibilities, she left the red wagon by the soda machines and grabbed a grocery cart. She had two hours until everyone would converge upon her, expecting a delicious dinner. She had an abundance of time, and yet she hurried inside as though chased by demons. Cooking demons.

Gripping the plastic handle of the metal cart, she strode to the produce section. Tomatoes, lettuce, avocado. She quickly snatched up the fresh vegetables and added them to the basket. What else? Ah yes. She turned the cart and headed to the international foods aisle, scanning the shelves for what she needed.

"Tara?" Grant's voice sounded behind her. "Is that you?"

Stopping, she looked over her shoulder and then angled her body to watch him approach. Goodness. How had she forgotten how ruggedly handsome he was? His lithe, easy gait carried him to her side in moments. She swallowed, aware of a tingling in her entire body as his gaze skimmed her head to toe and back to meet her nervous regard. What was he doing in the grocery? She was not ready to face him. Not prepared to experience the rush of awareness that overwhelmed her when he stood so close.

A wave of memory swept through her mind. Beginning with the instant she'd met him and sensed the potential for a deep connection with him. Then Paulette's revelation of his illness and why he'd ventured to the small town. She couldn't bear the thought of him suffering, so had chosen to heal him without his knowledge. Or anyone else's. Only, Paulette had guessed and confronted her after Grant had departed for his big city life. She'd hoped he'd stay away and not question the change in his health. What if he had found out what she'd done?

"Grant." She swallowed again, her voice weak and breathy. *Calm. Breathe.* She could be an adult and talk with another one. Even if he was the most alluring man on earth. "What brings you to town? I thought you didn't enjoy the quaintness of Roseville."

"Small towns have never interested me because too many people know too much about everybody else's business." He raised both brows as a smile hinted he recognized just how unsettled she was around him. "I'm only here to do a little sleuthing. Do you mind?"

Mind? Absolutely. "Of course not. How long will you stay?" *Really, Tara? How inane and rude can you be?* She must restore her composure, her equilibrium, or she'd mortify herself before the man. "I mean, how long will you be able to stay?"

"I'll leave after Thanksgiving. Head to the city and civilization." He glanced at the package of taco shells in her hands. "Is that for dinner tonight?"

Placing the box in the cart, she reached for a second one and added it to the growing pile. "Taco dinner is one of the few meals I can usually fix without incident."

Grant chuckled and rested his hands on the metal frame of the cart. "Sounds like you don't much enjoy cooking."

"We take turns, so I only have to do it a couple times a week." She shrugged and pushed the basket into motion, forcing Grant to straighten and walk beside her. Dawdling would limit the time she had to chop and dice and, worse, prolong the amount of time she'd be alone with him. "Simple fare is my specialty."

She paused to select bottles of mild and medium taco sauce and placed them into the basket. Pushing on, she slowed her pace when she saw a sudden roadblock ahead in the form of a mini family reunion. Annoyance shot through her. She needed to finish her shopping and retreat to her home, away from this man until her sisters could provide a buffer of sorts. His presence shook her to the core with awareness and longing. Beth had already as much as claimed him. As such, Tara wouldn't interfere with her older sister's choice. But that meant Tara must defend herself from his nearness.

"What kind of meat will you cook tonight?" He shot a sideways look her direction and then focused on the aisle ahead of them where the boisterous family had blocked their way.

She paused, waiting for the small group of animated people to notice her and Grant, and then with a word of thanks, she continued. Turning into the condiments aisle, she picked up the pace, skimming the bottles and cans of olives and pickles until spotting what she searched for. She selected a small can of sliced black olives and a can of sliced jalapenos. "Do you have a preference?"

Grant shook his head, watching her drop the cans into the cart. "What do you usually fix?"

She spun the cart around to head up the aisle toward the meat counter. Grant fell in beside her, much like a married couple. *Whoa. Get a grip.* She might be in a market but not in the market for a husband. And definitely not Grant. So stand down, libido, because the man beside her, no matter how lovely to look at and how smart, was not for her.

"Lean ground beef or chicken, most often. Sometimes I use steamed shrimp, but only when I'm feeling fancy."

"You know how to steam shrimp?" Grant tilted his head as he glanced at her. "That's impressive."

Her cheeks warmed at the unwarranted compliment, and a flush of pleasure swept through her. She wished. "No, I buy them already cooked."

"Keeps it simple, like you said, and yet still healthier than red meats." He smiled at her, taking control of the cart. "You lead, and I'll follow."

The brush of his hands on hers as they exchanged places made her gasp. Lordy, but he could stir her desires without a thought or effort on his part. She tamped down on her uncalled-for and unwanted reaction and took a calming breath. Letting it out slowly, she strode ahead of him, well aware of his eyes on her back, or more probably her backside. She sped up, wanting to as quickly as possible end the uncomfortable ordeal.

"I'm thinking lean beef tonight." She grabbed up a package of meat and pivoted to lay it in the cart. Her senses reeled when she inhaled his heady cologne. "Now to the dairy section, and then I'll be all done."

"After you." Grant waited for her to start walking, but she hesitated.

"Why are you here?" Tara placed one hand on the frame of the cart and held fast. Her curiosity won over her reluctance. "In Edna's, I mean?"

He pursed his lips as he glanced away and then returned to contemplate her for two heart beats. "My mother taught me never to tell a lie. The truth is that I saw you park your wagon out front and followed you."

"You're stalking me?" She blinked, clutching the basket more tightly. He'd made an effort to follow her, but for what purpose? He didn't seem the creepy kind of man. More the big, strong, smart, decadent pleasure of a man.

"No, no, no." He waved off her question with a wink. "I wanted to talk with you, that's all. Like we're doing."

"Why?" She folded her arms over her chest to stop her fingers from visibly trembling. Or reaching out to touch him, feel his hair in her hands. The electric current she knew existed between them. He activated all of her senses much like catnip for a feline. Drawing her toward him even as she pulled away from the attraction.

"Because I enjoyed dancing with you at the Halloween party last month and I wanted to thank you for making me feel so welcome." He didn't move, holding onto the handle with a loose grip as she gazed at him.

"You're welcome. But you could have told me that at dinner tonight." She sensed a growing unease on Grant's part and wondered at the cause. "You needn't follow me around town."

He shrugged, letting one hand release the cart as a slow smile replaced the cautious regard. "Not even if I enjoy the view?"

Heat washed her cheeks as she slowly shook her head. "Don't."

His smile grew as he studied her in silence for a few moments. "Why not?"

"Because…" How could she explain?

A hundred excuses raced through her mind. Each weaker than the last. The reasons she ardently denied her attraction to him remained location and her sister's prior claim to him. If they found being together pleasant, then why would she deny them? Besides, he lived hundreds of miles from her small town. From her sisters, more to the point. In a big city with all the culture and convenience that implied. He'd made it quite clear he had no desire to live in a backwater place like Roseville. He'd never trade his urban life to live in a quaint, historic town in the south. She couldn't imagine living surrounded by all the concrete, macadam, and glass. She'd visited big cities and quickly had become distressed by the abundance of people, smells, flashing lights. The noise in particular inundated her senses. Most importantly, her sisters lived in Roseville, so she would also. Until the day she died. No, they were entirely incompatible even if they were drawn to each other.

"Because why?" He continued to look at her with his dreamy eyes searching her face, her eyes.

"Never mind. Let's go." She spun, unwilling to share the fact that her desires were at war with the reality that he would leave and break her heart if she entrusted it to him while he visited. Better to let Beth have her shot at him since she had a more adventurous heart than Tara. Beth would likely welcome the chance to escape, a thought that chilled Tara's heart. Separation from her sisters? She certainly hoped not but unlike Beth, she couldn't see into the future. Marching the length of the store to the refrigerated section, she could feel the weight of his gaze. Finally, she snatched a container of sour cream and a package of shredded cheddar cheese, tossed them into the basket to avoid contact with him, and hurried toward the checkout.

She needed to keep some bulwark between herself and the man following her. Prevent herself from succumbing to the temptation he represented to her sense of wellbeing. For her own and Beth's sake.

Grant trailed after her, keeping pace with her frantic flight despite the metal cart rattling behind her. He remained silent except for a light chuckle every few strides. Let him laugh. She needed time and distance from him.

When they reached the checkout line with its black conveyor belt, Tara greeted the clerk and then addressed Grant. "I can manage from here. I'll see you in a bit at the house. Okay?"

"Actually, can I give you a lift home? I'm not sure where you live."

"Well…" She noticed the clerk waiting, and started removing items from the basket and slapping them onto the moving belt. All the while her heart raced at the mere idea of being alone with him. In his car. In her home. "Use the GPS on your phone."

"I'll stay out of your way." He held up one hand; two fingers pointed to the ceiling as if he were a Boy Scout. "I promise."

"I—" She was torn between longing and fear. Between wanting to spend more time with him and the fear he'd break her if she did. She opened her mouth to object, saw the twinkle in his eyes, the gentle smile and then he winked at her. Clever man. *Fine.* She huffed away her resistance. "Okay."

Cheeks flaming, she reached for the lettuce only to have his hand bump into hers as he claimed it. Her gaze flew to his, connected for several rapid breaths, and then she grabbed the head of lettuce and put it on the conveyor. Severing the sensation sweeping through her. The clerk's expression hinted she suspected what had occurred between them, but she merely smiled and continued scanning items with a steady *beep, beep, beep.*

"Awesome." Grant handed her the last item, which she carefully removed from his hand. "I'm parked in front of the wine shop."

She tossed him a look as she handed her credit card to the clerk who regarded her with humor in her eyes. "Why over there?"

"My contribution to dinner." He pushed the cart

through the line so the bagger could place the filled bags into it.

Taking her card, Tara slipped it into her wallet. Noted the last bag had been put into the cart and Grant waited for her to follow him. To his car. Then to her home. She swallowed the lump in her throat and squared her shoulders. She could do this. She hoped.

Chapter Four

Grant leaned on the grocery cart near the automatic door, waiting for Tara to stop staring at him with a hint of doe in the headlights in her eyes. He liked the fact that she reacted to his presence, so much so he'd decided to invite himself to her house earlier than originally planned. It hadn't been his intention to horn in on her, but hey, he was a man, and he liked what he saw. When they'd danced together, he had been attracted to her but didn't pursue anything more then because of the prognosis he'd been facing. But with the change in his health, and in his plans for his future, he was ready to explore his options. He had her address, but he needed an excuse to keep her at his side. She intrigued him, not only because she appeared reluctant and nervous in his company, intimating her returned interest despite her self-denial of the attraction she apparently had for him. But also because her eyes fairly glowed when she looked at him, lips slightly parted and oh so tempting.

Tara soon recovered and started walking his direction. He led the way out of Edna's. Grant strode to his car and popped open the trunk with the key fob button. Metallic rattling sounded behind him as he placed the first bag into the depths of the trunk. He looked over his shoulder, bending a tad sideways to see behind him. Tara stopped with the little wagon in tow.

"Oh good." Grant straightened and turned to pick up the wagon and then ease it into the trunk alongside the lone grocery sack. "I'm glad you remembered."

"I could never leave it behind." Tara lifted a plastic sack from the cart and handed it to him. "In any case, everyone knows it's mine and would have left it there until I retrieved it."

"Why a wagon?"

"It's one I've had since I was little, and I like it." She offered him another sack of groceries. "Why waste it when it has so many memories attached?"

"Good point." Grant took the bag, pleased at her small startle when his fingers intentionally brushed hers. "Roseville is a nice town, where people look out for one another."

She gazed up at him with wide eyes for a moment and then glanced away, scanning the area around the grocery store. "I'm surprised you noticed. I didn't think you cared for Roseville."

He deposited the bag in the trunk and closed the lid. "Why?"

"You seem more attuned to the urban scene." She shrugged and followed him to the passenger side of the car.

"The city is where I've felt at home." At least until recent events shed new light on his life. A quick scan of the parking lot showed the difference in locale with the quantity of pickup trucks of varying sizes. The country life seemed to sprout more rednecks than his hometown. Indeed, he found himself appreciating the slower pace and easy-going nature of the people. He pulled open the door and held it for her to slip into the car. "Where I'm from the smaller acts of kindness are not as evident because there are so many people living in the city compared to a small town."

"So more clutter to block how people act with each other?" Tara grasped the seat buckle and pulled it across her to snap it into place. Then she studied him for a second before grinning. "Easier in a small town with fewer people to see patterns in the layers of society?"

"Like strata in a cutaway, those rock walls the highway goes between when you're driving down the interstate." He liked her sense of humor, the way she viewed the world around her. At her nod, he pushed the door shut, then hurried around to the driver's side. Turning the engine on, he glanced at her. "Which way?"

"Take a right out of the parking lot." Tara pointed to where he should go. "It's just a couple blocks east."

Grant navigated through the traffic around the town square, noting the historic nature of the downtown and the friendly greetings exchanged by the people passing each other on the sidewalk. He'd disparaged the town when he and Zak had first arrived, but things had changed. Like his opinion and sensibilities of what proved important. Soon he turned into the driveway of the Golden sisters' house, one of the more elegant historic homes. "Nice place."

Unfastening her seatbelt, Tara reached to open the door but paused to let her gaze skim over the abode. "We love living here. I can't imagine ever living anywhere else."

"If it's where you grew up, that makes perfect sense." The Victorian house boasted the requisite wraparound porch and gingerbread woodworking. Pale yellow walls provided a background for the chocolate trim around the many windows and the front door. Flowering bushes and stately trees added a touch of nature to soften the setting. Overall the kind of place he wouldn't mind living in one day, after he'd found the right woman and a more interesting job. The longer he spent away from the lab, the lighter his heart felt. "It's your home."

Tara pushed her door open, and Grant followed suit. He popped open the trunk, pulled out the wagon and then grabbed a sack. Moments later they had the groceries in the wagon, and Tara pulled it along a brick sidewalk flanked by flower beds toward the rear of the house. Grant slammed the lid closed and hurried to catch up with her as she parked the wagon on the back porch and unlocked the door. She grabbed both bags and went inside, Grant trailing after her. The kitchen stood empty and silent as he stepped inside and eased the door closed. Cozy and compact. A kitchen ready for experienced hands to create something fabulous. A real working kitchen with a center island waiting to be used to fix hearty meals. He inhaled and caught the lingering odor of singed sugar and cinnamon, making his mouth water. Despite his tendency to choose speed over scratch made, he enjoyed cooking on occasion. He wanted to roll up his sleeves and get busy.

"I like your kitchen." He sidestepped so she could walk past him, aiming for the pantry. "I bet it's easy to work in."

"Yes, but there's little counter space. I wish it were bigger." She yanked open the pantry door with one hand and placed the boxes of shells inside with the other. "Mom made sure of that when she updated the kitchen ten years ago."

"Your mom liked to cook?" Grant could imagine his mother would approve of the layout of the open counter space, the placement of the range and microwave, the fridge and dishwasher. She'd agree on the lack of work space, but there seemed to be enough to manage.

"She was a wizard in the kitchen. When I was very little, she'd pull me in my wagon down to the grocery store, and I'd help her select the fresh produce and the meats for the meals she'd fix." Her gaze turned inward, a small smile hinting at the fond memories she recalled. Another darker emotion flashed across her face and then disappeared. "Then I'd walk beside her with the treasure in the wagon all the way home."

"Treasure?" He grinned at her, enjoying her tale even while pondering if he'd imagined the flicker in her expression.

She chuckled briefly and then sobered. "That's what I thought it was at the time." She shook her head. "I didn't realize what an enchanted period of my life I was living."

"How so?" He shifted to stand closer to her, within reach of her hand if he chose to take hold of her long fingers.

"Mom made me feel special and loved and protected all wrapped up in one package." She rested her hands on the counter in front of her, her gaze flitting about the room. "I miss her so much and yet feel her near me at times. Like she's keeping an eye on me still."

"You are special, and loved, and I'd bet protected, even if you don't see it yourself." He wrapped a lock of her hair around one finger, marveling at the rich texture.

She blinked up at him, her lustrous hazel eyes quizzical. "Why do you say that?"

"You have two sisters and now your cousins who all care about you." Releasing her hair, he studied her lovely features, her pert nose, tear-filled eyes, and bow-shaped mouth. "And you have Zak and Max who also are there for you. You're a lucky woman, Tara."

"That's one way to look at it, I suppose." She dashed her hand over her eyes, remnants of her tears spattered on her high cheek bones. "Somehow it feels more like I'm facing the world on my own, wanting to but not quite meeting the mark of success."

"Why so?" He frowned, trying but failing to follow her reasoning. From his point of view, she had everything. She was smart, talented, a successful businesswoman. Beautiful, too. "I don't understand."

She waved him off, her tears drying as her gaze shifted to stare at the range. "Never mind."

"You're also lucky to have such a fine place to cook." He surveyed the kitchen and then leveled his regard on her. "This kitchen is compact, and that makes everything within easy reach."

"You sound like Beth. She's always going on about the utility and efficiency." Rolling those same tantalizing eyes, she shook her head and spun around to finish stashing what she called her treasure. "Do you know how to cook, too?"

"A little." He stepped out of her way with a chuckle. "I'm a bachelor. I don't always cook, but I know how."

"So you eat a lot of take-out." With a few efficient moves, she had everything put away. She consulted her watch and then speared him with her gaze. "Is that right?"

"Spot on." Grant chuckled and sidestepped to the end of the counter to give her more space. "But I prefer home-cooked when I can get it."

"We have a little while until Roxie and Beth are home for dinner." She regarded him steadily for a moment. "What do you want to do while we wait?"

Ideas abounded as to what he'd like to do with her, but the timing most definitely was not right. Nor would she agree with his suggestions in that vein. They hardly knew one another. "It's a nice afternoon. Do you have a book I could read outside?"

She nodded and strode across the floor to a bookshelf in the corner. "We do own a bookstore, you know."

He crossed the room to see what tomes stood on the four shelves. Perusing the titles, he was surprised by the eclectic array of topics and genres. High-brow fiction. Mysteries. Romances. Science fiction. Some nonfiction and even an essay collection.

"That's quite a mix." He spotted a new edition of Edgar Allan Poe's work and reached for it. "Okay if I read this one?"

She drew in a quick breath and raised one brow, surprise in her eyes. "Sure. We bring home a selection of new releases to read so we can hand-sell to our customers."

"Nice perk of your job." Grant wondered at her reaction to his request. He glanced from her to the hardback, opening it to determine the contents. Sure enough, the editors had included his favorite poem, "The Raven." He closed the book and caught her studying him. "I'd spend all my time reading if I worked in a bookstore."

"It is quite tempting." Tara moved away from the shelves to stand by the table, the tips of the fingers on her right hand resting lightly on its surface. Such refined digits, too. He nearly reached for her hand, but she lifted hers and slipped them into her front jeans pockets. "There's a grouping of chairs outside. You go on out as I need to start dinner."

"Come join me if you have a few minutes." He contemplated the disbelief reflected in her countenance. "What? I enjoy talking with you."

She bit her lip and then moistened her lower lip with her tongue. The movement caught his attention, made him wonder what it would be like to kiss her. An event he hoped would happen before long. Wide-eyed, she stared at him, almost as though she read his thoughts, sensed the desire he felt for her without him having to say a word.

She studied him for a beat. "I can't promise I'll have time."

"That's okay, since I pushed my way into your afternoon." He took one last look at her tempting lips and then forced himself to walk to the door. Away from the woman sparking desires both familiar and foreign. He'd never thought so frequently about settling down, of finding a wife, one day having kids. Since the tumor, though, his goals in life had shifted to include more personal achievements versus professional ones. Still, neither of them was ready to commit to anything smacking of a relationship let alone physical intimacy. But he relished spending time with the seductress. "I'll leave you to your work."

As he closed the door behind him, he chuckled to himself at Tara's long sigh of relief. He paused at the edge of the porch, letting his gaze drift over the landscaped yard. A privacy fence marked the extent of the property, its slatted boards supporting several types of dormant climbing vines and roses. Stepping stones wound across the space, leading to a circular brick patio in the far corner. Four chairs surrounded a covered fire pit, inviting him to venture down the steps and along the flat slabs of stone. Choosing the chair facing the house, he rested the book on his leg while he took note of the apparent effort expended on creating a comfy and welcoming place.

Flower beds edged with brick complemented the patio. Pampas grass mingled with what would be flowering bushes come spring. He could identify roses and azaleas from the shape of their leaves but several other varieties dotted the small yet beautiful yard. Off to one side, a brick grill snuggled up to a garden shed with a workbench under an overhanging roof. Come springtime, they'd have an oasis to escape to after work.

He raised his gaze to peruse the back of the historic home. Signs of wear and age in the form of peeling paint and warped shutters had him itching for the proper tools to mend the damage. Three women living in such a large old house would have a difficult time keeping up with the attendant care and maintenance. Overall the home showed they worked to preserve it as best they could, but if they had a man around to help... He blinked and gripped the book as a sudden thought darted through his mind. He toyed with the idea only for a moment then dismissed it as absurd.

Shaking his head at the rash idea of moving to such a small town when his work and his home remained in the city light years away in both distance and culture, he opened the book and began to read.

Chapter Five

Only a little while longer and she'd be saved. Her sisters would return home and she wouldn't be faced with confronting the one man she must resist. She had to avoid Grant and the strong desire, the compulsion to touch him, make contact with him in any way possible, that she experienced whenever he stood near. Yet she remained hyper aware of him sitting in her yard reading one of her beloved authors. How had he zeroed in on that particular book so fast? A sign? She hoped not. Staring at him sitting so casually in her favorite chair wouldn't help either. Pacing away from the window, she pulled the band out of her ponytail and ran her fingers through her hair, disentangling the tresses but not her thoughts.

Deciding action suited the situation better than contemplating the hunk in her yard, she set to work preparing to make dinner. Soon she had the fresh veggies washed and ready to dice and slice. She cut up a clove of garlic and a small yellow onion, sniffling and wiping at her tears with the back of her hand. Adding the ground beef to a skillet, she scraped the onion and garlic off the cutting board into the pan, ready to cook later. As she turned to pull bowls out to hold the various ingredients, the door opened and Beth sauntered inside, moving with care as she shut the door with a mumbled greeting. The squinting eyes beneath a furrowed brow gave Tara the answer as to the reason.

"Headache?" Tara went to bolster Beth with a supportive arm around her waist. "Are you okay?"

"Migraine." Beth rubbed her temples with her fingers. "Second one this week."

"Here, sit on this chair, and I'll help you." Tara guided her to the straight-backed chair beside the table. "Did you take anything for it?"

"No. I came home to you." She sank onto the seat with a groan, her eyes half closed. "I hate being ill."

"What triggered it this time?" Tara stood behind her sister and rested her hands on Beth's shoulders, probing for the location of the headache. "Any idea?"

"People." Beth leaned her head back, eyes closed, a hand rubbing her forehead. "Damn town."

Tara peered at her for several long moments. "What do you mean? Did something happen at the store?"

"Nothing ever happens in this town." Beth opened her eyes halfway, pain evident in the dullness in them. "One of these days I'm going to leave and never come back. There has to be more to life than Roseville."

"Never?" The mere hint of such an occurrence shot alarm through Tara. To never see her sister again? "You don't mean that, surely."

How could she protect her sister from pain and illness if she moved away? Flashes of fear and despair appeared in her mind's eye at the idea. She'd have to find a way to monitor her. Skype? Other social media? Not good enough. Proximity played an important role in sensing how she could best help them.

"No. I'd probably come to visit." Beth lowered her eyelids again as she grimaced. "Do your thing, sis."

"Relax and focus on a pleasant place." Tara placed her hands on either side of Beth's head, resting them above her ears as she closed her own eyes to concentrate. Pinpointed the pain center and began to draw it away and out of Beth's skull.

Grant strode into the kitchen bringing the scents of the outdoors into the small space. He hesitated at the door, the new annotated edition of Poe's writings tucked under one arm. "What are you doing?"

Tara ran her hands over and around Beth's head for another moment or two. Then dropped her hands to her sides as she stared at the man. Talk about timing. His was impeccable for interrupting. She rubbed her palms together as she considered an appropriate response that wasn't a lie but not the whole truth. "Massaging Beth's headache away." She glanced at her sister. "Why don't you go on into your room, and I'll be there shortly."

Beth nodded and rose to walk slowly out of the room without a backward glance or a word. Tara wanted to follow, ensure the pain had ended, but first she had to put any suspicions Grant may have to rest. She turned to face him and relief washed over her at his open countenance.

"How is she feeling?" Grant claimed her attention, his gaze locked with hers. "She didn't seem right when she passed me."

"You noticed?" Another mark in his favor. Damn him.

"That's why I came in. It was pretty obvious, even from a distance." He claimed the chair, turning it around so he could rest his elbows on the back, and propped his head in his hands. "Even for a guy like me."

"Thanks for asking about her. She gets migraines occasionally, but a little shut-eye and her…treatment, and she'll be up and around again in no time. I'll check on her when I finish cutting up these veggies." She motioned with the knife at the duo of bright red beefsteak tomatoes sitting beside the cutting board.

"I could do that while you tend to her, if you'd like." Grant stared at her, moving his hands to brace them on the chair, prepared to stand with her agreement.

The challenge she faced was in fixing anything in the kitchen without a disaster occurring. But she had to do it herself, not let somebody else step in and take over. Much as she'd rather have someone else do the cooking so she need not embarrass herself on a regular basis. But Roxie was right. She had to overcome whatever made it impossible for her to succeed in the kitchen.

She shook her head and reached for the first tomato. "Not necessary, but thanks. This won't take but a few minutes."

"Then I'm just in time to watch you make dinner." He settled into a comfortable position and waited with an expectant expression plastered on his face. "Perfect timing."

Oh, Mother, may I. Tara's hand shook, the knife dropping to the cutting board. A good thing as she could easily cut herself otherwise. Retrieving the knife, she gripped it to force calm inside her churning stomach. All the man had to do was walk in and look at her to make her on edge and hyper aware of him. No way would she let him know the effect he had on her equilibrium and self-respect. She drew in a long breath as she straightened her spine, steeling herself to deny her wayward response to his presence. Her plan waited to be put into motion.

"Not much to see." Unsure whether she could handle the slippery tomatoes in her present state, Tara grabbed the head of lettuce and sliced it into shreds, tossing handfuls into a waiting bowl. Or attempting to. Bits of lettuce spewed across the counter. Snatching them up, she flung the shreds into the bowl and then attacked the head of lettuce again. "I don't usually have an audience."

"Am I making you uncomfortable?" Grant grinned at her, his expression both friendly and smug. "I can leave if you'd prefer."

And have him think he'd elicited a physical response from her? Even if he were correct? What a stroke to his ego that would be. "No, it's fine. Tell me what you think of the book."

She continued to slice and dice while Grant watched. Tried to ignore the way his gaze followed the movement of her hands as if mesmerized by her long fingers splayed over the avocado. She sliced it in half, removed the pit, and then began peeling the skin away to reveal the green flesh. She tried to not react to his intent regard which sparked heat in her center, a flicker growing into a flame of desire to have his full attention.

"The editors did a pretty good job of providing the context for the stories. Especially in explaining the allusions in 'The Raven'." He shrugged as his lips parted slightly when she began cutting the avocado into bite-sized pieces and placed them in a separate bowl. "You make that look so easy."

She met his gaze and then wished she'd kept her eyes on the cutting board. The intensity of his eyes watching her sent thrills of yearning spiraling into her core. Added fuel to the flames of desire already flickering to life. She couldn't permit herself to fall for him. She wouldn't. Time for redirection. "Beth is a whiz in the kitchen. She puts me to shame."

She selected a tomato and started dicing it. His silent perusal disrupted her usual precise strokes, reducing her slices to awkward chunks instead of the small squares she'd aimed to make. It would have to do. She sighed inwardly so Grant wouldn't suspect how discombobulated his being so close made her feel. Pulling off a decent meal with an appealing presentation remained her primary goal. Secondly, to do so without making a fool of herself.

Grant turned at a sound in the hallway. "Look who's feeling better."

Beth sauntered into the kitchen, a slight smile gracing her lips. "Sorry I didn't say hello earlier."

"No problem. I could tell you weren't your usual cheery

self." He pushed to his feet and turned the chair around with a flip of his hands. "Have a seat."

"You didn't need to do that." Beth accepted the invitation, crossing her legs as she smiled up at Grant. "But thanks."

"You look like you feel much better." The fact he'd acted the gentleman didn't escape her notice. Drat the man. Tara scraped the last of the diced tomato into another bowl and then crossed to the sink to wash her hands. Drying them on a towel, she turned to inspect her sister's features for any signs of distress or pain. "I'm glad you're back on your feet."

"I didn't want to miss out on your dinner this evening." She tossed a glance up at Grant, where he leaned against the counter. "Especially with our esteemed guest."

Good. Beth continued to be interested in Grant. Tara could step away and encourage them to explore their likes and dislikes, their similarities and differences. Ultimately for Beth and Grant to fall in love and move away, which would satisfy all three of them. The plan would work. Despite the clawing jealousy bursting to life inside by the simple thought. She squared her shoulders, prepared to fight her own inclinations for everyone's sanity.

"Beth, if you're feeling up to it, why don't you take Grant on the nickel tour of the house?" Spend some time together and get him out of here, is what she really wanted to say. Before she succumbed to the temptations he embodied. "Grant hasn't seen it yet."

"I'd like that." He pushed away from the counter and offered a hand to Beth to help her stand. "If you don't mind, that is."

Beth took his proffered hand and rose to her feet. She started and then flicked a surprised look at Tara for a heartbeat. Turning back to Grant, she angled her head with a smug smile. "Follow my lead."

"Be sure to tell him the history behind the dining room

table. That's a great story." Tara lifted both brows as she speared her sister with her gaze. "And the horses."

Grant shot her a glance, brows raised. "Horses?"

"Right. We'll get to that. Our grandfather liked to work with his hands and made furniture. He converted a baby grand piano into the most amazing table." Beth pivoted and sauntered out of the kitchen, in tour guide mode, with Grant beside her. "Come on; you'll like this."

Tara had a moment of triumph after they left the kitchen, Beth's voice fading as they made their way through the house. Roxie would come home in a few minutes, so Tara turned to start the meat to cook. She retrieved the boxes of shells and then turned the oven on to preheat. Pulling a sheet pan from the cabinet beside the stove, she banged it onto the counter as the door opened and Roxie sashayed inside.

"Hey, is that Grant's car out front?" Roxie placed her purse on the shelf by the door and stuffed her keys inside. "I wasn't expecting him until a little later."

Tension in Roxie's shoulders hinted at a difficult day at the store. With the busy holiday season about to descend upon the popular book and gift store, more customers also meant the need for more stock and patience to deal with the sometimes rushed, gruff, or even rude people. Roxie had amazing people skills, friendly and welcoming, but when too many of the latter type of people invaded the tranquility of the Golden Owl, her nerves ended up raw by the time she returned home. Perhaps Tara had stumbled on the cause of Beth's distress as well.

"He drove me home from Edna's earlier this afternoon." Tara opened the box and removed the shells, arranging them on the pan as she glanced at her sister. "He's been hanging out with me."

"Lucky you." Roxie winked at her and then rolled her shoulders a few times before crossing the room to peer at the bowls of tomato, avocado, and lettuce. "Want me to do anything?"

Tara studied her sister's tired expression and then returned to the task at hand. "Nope. Dinner will be in about ten minutes, so you have time to freshen up if you'd like." She arranged the second set of shells beside the first before turning to stir the sizzling meat and onion. "Beth is giving Grant the tour."

"Oh good. This old house has quite a history; one people need to remember." Roxie nodded to herself as she walked across the room. "I'll be back in a few minutes."

Tara pivoted to open the cans of olives and peppers. Draining the excess liquid in the sink, she dumped the contents of each into separate ramekin bowls. While the meat cooked, she carried the bowls to the table and arrayed them in the center. Then she hurried to grab the pan of shells and pop them into the oven to warm for a few minutes. She spun around when she heard Grant's booming laughter in the hallway, footsteps drawing near. Her pulse quick-stepped in her veins.

"So they stabled the horses in the basement during the war? That's incredible." Grant's rich, dark-chocolate voice held admiration as he walked beside Beth into the kitchen. "And outrageous to boot."

"Did you show him the scrapes on the stones from the horses' metal shoes?" Roxie trailed behind them, her long brown hair confined in a loose bun at the back of her head. "I find it fun to imagine what it must have been like, what it must have smelled and sounded like to have horses in the basement."

Tara laughed at the shock on Grant's face. "What, Grant? You didn't think about the smell?"

He met her gaze and shook his head slowly. "Awful. Just awful."

They all laughed at his expression. Tara liked his easy

manner, the way he fit into the group without fanfare or obvious effort. He didn't need to be the center of attention even though in this instance his status as a guest made him their focus. She smiled at him, especially when he offered to help Beth set the table. Roxie took drink orders and filled glasses with beer or wine as each requested. Tara lifted the lid off the skillet and stirred the meat, pleased all the elements of the meal would finish at the same time. She set the lid on a cold burner, turned off the heat under the skillet, and then drained the meat before pouring it into a large bowl. Carrying the steaming bowl to the table, she sniffed. Was something burning?

Oh no. Not again. She thumped the bowl onto the table and then whirled around. Unlike the sticky buns earlier in the morning, the shells were not just singed but on frigging damn fire. Flames flickered inside the closed oven, smoke seeping out and setting off the damn alarm. Yet again.

She ran toward the oven, but Grant sprinted to reach the stove first. He yanked open the door and grabbed the lid, slamming it on the shells to smother the flames. Tara stared in horror at the sight of the crushed and charred shells, a sight that only made the smell of burned corn worse, choking everyone and making them cough, combined with the sound of the blaring smoke alarm Roxie frantically fanned with a towel.

"I've never seen taco shells ignite before." Grant used pot holders to lift the pan out of the oven and put it on top of the stove. Closing the oven door, he turned off the heat. "What happened?"

"I have no clue." Tara glared at the ruined mess. "I've never had them burst into flames. Ever." She crossed her arms and glanced at Grant, then Beth, and finally Roxie. How was she to salvage this disaster? All the toppings but no shells. "Taco salad without the tacos, anyone?"

Roxie's giggle grew into a chuckle and then exploded

into guffaws. Her laughter proved contagious, and soon everyone but Tara was wiping tears from their eyes as they tried to regain control.

After several minutes, Tara clapped her hands sharply and glared at each of them, which brought their laughing fit to an abrupt halt. "I don't find this situation funny."

"We're not laughing at you, sis. But you must admit it is rather ironic." Roxie dried her eyes as she smiled at Tara. "Besides, it's not a total loss. We can always eat the other stuff nachos style."

"Sure. I'll grab the chips." Beth hurried to the pantry and pulled out the bag. "Let's eat."

Grant smiled kindly at Tara, which only served to make her more embarrassed at this unprecedented failure. "No worries, Tara. Everything else looks really good."

"You have to say that since you're the guest." She sidled past him to take her seat, avoiding any possible contact as discreetly as possible. "Why don't you sit beside Beth and I'll sit over here." Across the table, as far away as she could position herself.

He winked at her as he did as she instructed. "Fine by me."

Was that a smirk on his face? Why? It didn't matter. She planned to push him toward her sister at every turn. Encourage the two of them to fall in love, marry, and move away. Her stomach fell as a shiver shimmied up her spine. Never mind. She'd grow accustomed to the idea over time. She smoothed a paper napkin into her lap before piling chips on her plate. She looked up and then froze when she understood why he acted like he'd won first prize. She sat directly across from him so that every time she lifted her gaze she'd be totally aware of the gorgeous man she most wanted to avoid. She looked to her plate, intent on ignoring him as best she could.

Dinner couldn't end soon enough.

Chapter Six

*R*ain drummed on the roof of the house, matching Tara's mood. Dark, dismal, wet. Perfect. She rolled out of bed and padded to the bathroom to start her day. With luck, nobody would mention the fire. Mortified by the extreme kindness radiating from Grant in her direction all through dinner had left her feeling irritable. After she finished her morning routine and dressed in forest green leggings and a bulky sweater, she headed to the kitchen for coffee.

She didn't blame Grant for not sticking around very long after the meal. After all, she avoided eye contact with him the entire time he sat across from her, tempting her to meet his gaze. What an awful, embarrassing evening too.

When she strolled into the kitchen, Beth glanced up from the newspaper she read at the table. "Morning, sunshine."

"Not likely." Tara shot her a grimace as she opened the cabinet to select a mug. "Please don't mention it."

"What?" Beth blinked wide eyes in a failed attempt to feign innocence.

"Just drop it." Tara poured hot brew into her cup and replaced the carafe. Holding the mug with both hands, she took a sip while Beth chuckled and returned her attention to the article she'd been perusing. A change of subject. That's what she needed. "What are you reading?"

Beth pointed a finger at the text, tracking where she read. "Seems there was a mild earthquake centered about thirty miles from here up on the plateau. A known fault line but usually inactive, according to this. So the quake was a surprise."

"So far out there won't be any damage or injury." Tara sipped and contemplated her sister's sudden interest in geology. Promising. *Upsetting*, a little voice whispered. She ignored it. "At least it wasn't strong enough for us to feel it."

"Which is a huge relief to me." Roxie strode into the room, the scent of her perfume vying with the aroma of the coffee.

Tara peered at Roxie, surprised and amazed at how sharp her ears must be to add to an ongoing conversation immediately upon entrance into the room. "Why is that?"

"I've made a decision, and I don't want anything to interfere with it." Roxie filled a mug in several swift moves and then leaned against the counter to address Tara and Beth. She slowly smiled, her gaze resting on Tara for several moments. "It's something I think will help you, in particular. Guess what it is."

Roxie's expression hinted at mischief by the glint in her eyes and the upward tilt of her lips. A slight flush also indicated heightened excitement along with the small opening of her mouth as she waited for them to follow her lead. The longer Tara looked at her, the more certain she became she wasn't going to like her decision.

Tara studied her, finally realizing she'd stared too long. "Must we play games so early in the morning?"

"Spill it, Roxie." Beth turned the page of the paper but kept her attention on the conversation instead of the headlines, one hand laying on the newsprint. "Neither of us are in the mood to guess."

"You guys are no fun this morning." Roxie shook her head and shook a finger at them. "Fine. I'll just tell you. We're going to throw a good old-fashioned Thanksgiving dinner."

Tara's heart nearly stopped at the idea. The three of them in the kitchen together? Panic filled her chest, beginning as a flutter and slowly expanding into a swarm of agitated butterflies frolicking inside. "We are?"

"Don't worry. I'll take care of the hard stuff. You know, the turkey, dressing, mashed potatoes, and gravy." Roxie pinned Beth with a look and continued. "You can take care of the green bean casserole, candied yams, glazed carrots, and whatever other veggies you choose." Those hazel eyes landed on Tara. "All you have to do is make desserts. Whatever kinds of pies or cakes you'd like. Easy peasy."

"But—" She couldn't. The chaos in her chest increased and consumed her. She didn't want to bake, let alone make a cake. Pressure built in her chest, her heart skipping a beat now and again. Then she remembered the Sweet Serendipity and relaxed with a heartfelt sigh. She didn't have to bake anything. "Thank goodness for the new bakery."

Roxie wagged a finger at her, her gaze sharp and unbending. "Nope. We're making everything ourselves, just like Mom used to do. It's a family tradition."

The tradition was their mother made everything, and they assisted. Tara had mainly contributed by helping with the shopping and on the big day setting the table. Not by actually chopping or blending or whipping. A shudder of despair vibrated along her spine as she blinked at her sisters. Tears slid unheeded down her cheeks. She imagined globs instead of batter, lumps instead of whipped. All the ways she would mangle the act of preparing a dish that would prove both pleasing to the eye and edible. Very high thresholds indeed.

"Why would we go through the effort for the three of us?" Beth looked at Roxie, a double crease of confusion between her eyes.

"Good question, Beth." Tara smiled at her. She'd provided a potential out to dissuade Roxie from pursuing her crazy idea. "We don't need to have all that food for us."

"I forgot the best part." Roxie glanced at each of them, her eyes twinkling. "We won't invite our neighbors like we used to, but we will still have a full table. We're going to invite our cousins."

Cousins. Oh goodness, how soon she forgot they had new kin. Tara quickly ran through the recent revelations about their cousins. Meredith and Paulette O'Connell were found to be related to the three sisters, thanks to an indiscretion on the part of a shared grandfather. Tara liked them as friends even before they'd learned of their kinship, so adding the two ladies to the family had been a welcome event. She just hadn't thought about including them in their family holidays. Indeed, the dynamics of all of their family gatherings would change. A bittersweet thought as it meant absorbing new traditions into their existing ones. What traditions did they have that may need to be learned? Another impending change.

"What about Zak and Max?" Beth set her coffee on the table and then stood. "We're inviting them, too?"

"Naturally." Roxie dropped her hands from her hips and picked up her coffee to take a sip. "They're family by marriage."

The number of guests kept growing. Tara cringed inwardly at the dawning of another possible guest. Given he drove all those miles to spend the holiday with Zak, she had no doubt he'd end up sitting at their dining room table. Joy. "I have no idea what I'll make for dessert, though. Are you sure you don't want me to put together a nice salad? That would be healthier than all the sugars and fats in the desserts."

Roxie stared at her, slowly blinking both eyes. "Salad? Are you kidding me? At our first full family holiday dinner?"

Roxie's disappointed gaze chilled Tara to the core. Thanksgiving dinner had always been about the bounty of the harvest with a wide array of delicious temptations. Salad not among them. Ever. Tara swallowed and braced her shoulders. She'd make something for dessert. Something amazing and wonderful that wouldn't bring back the disappointment in Roxie's eyes. She couldn't stand to fail her big sister in her quest to bring the entire family together officially for the holiday banquet. Especially since it would be the first time with company since their mother's death.

She thought back over the years, trying to recall what her mother had fixed. Carrot cake with cream cheese frosting and walnuts sprinkled across the top? Her mouth watered at the idea but she couldn't do it. That was a recipe she and her mom had made together, not one she felt confident to make on her own. Angel food Waldorf cake? Way too complicated for her. Raisin cake? She saw again the result of her last attempt. A gooey mess. No, probably not a good idea. Strawberry rhubarb pie? How did one make a pie crust from scratch? She cringed. Each idea she dismissed as too complicated, but surely she could find something even a klutz could make.

"Fine. I'll do it, but under duress." Tara smothered a sigh as she turned to refill her cup, ignoring the slight tremor in her fingers as she poured the hot liquid.

Roxie chuckled and then cleared her throat. "One more thing, Beth."

At the sound of suppressed mirth in her oldest sister's voice, Tara slowly raised her eyes to determine what the cause might be. She soon found out.

"Yes, Roxie?" Beth drained her cup and set it on the table.

"Be sure to invite Grant, since he's in town." Roxie kept

her gaze on Tara even as she addressed the middle sister. "I'm sure he'd enjoy spending the day with us."

"Glad to." Beth smiled, glancing between Roxie and Tara for a moment or two. "He's quite a catch for the right lady."

The second proverbial shoe had hit the floor. Still, there was something off about Roxie's division of labor. Roxie knew Tara could pull together veggies much more easily than a fickle cake or the complexity of making pie crust. Whoever said pie was easy to make simply lied. There could be no other explanation. She caught Roxie's attention.

"You know I don't like to bake. Why are you pushing me into doing so?" Tara bit her lip, worrying it between her teeth as she waited for Roxie's response.

Roxie crossed her arms over her chest and raised one brow. "Consider it my challenge to you to work past the mental barrier you've erected on your ability to make a pie. Or a cake for that matter. I believe you can succeed. Don't you?"

Short answer? No. But she also never relished the feeling when her oldest sister, whom she had revered since she was a little girl in need of protection from her classmates, thought she wasn't doing her best. Roxie had gone to bat for her, defending Tara at recess and walking home from school from the sneers and jibes of the other kids. Seeing Roxie gazing at her with such deep disappointment made her squirm like a child in church and thus even more desirous to meet her sister's expectations. No matter what it took.

Tara attempted to smile at Roxie but imagined it looked rather wilted. "Never mind. I'll figure out something."

Chapter Seven

*L*ate fall afternoons in Tennessee proved hotter than anticipated. Grant swiped a hand across his brow to dry the sweat beading there from his efforts with the shovel. Clearing away the sod to create the walking path for the new memorial garden at Twin Oaks plantation gave him an excuse to be outside. To clear his head from the longing to find the woman who seemed to be in his every waking thought as well as in his dreams. He needed to focus on his mission. The reason why he came to Roseville in the first place. To find the source of the cure for the tumors that threatened his sight. To prove to his doctors it wasn't a miracle but could be explained using science. Like his dad always said, everything had a basis in cause and effect, in fact and experience. What others termed magical and mystical occurrences simply hadn't been scientifically explained yet. Well, he was going to find the answer to his question or die trying.

Although he'd already mystified them by contracting meningioma, a rare disease in itself and even more rarely found in men. They'd scrambled to try to understand how the disease had been introduced into his system, causing tumors to wrap around his optic nerves in such a way as to prohibit surgical removal without impairing or obliterating his sight. Without vision, he could not continue to be a geologist. His career would have ended along with his income. To say he had been scared and worried was an understatement. Zak had persuaded him to take a road trip with him, a totally unrealistic plan to use alchemy to cure him. He'd only agreed to travel to the backwater town of Roseville so that he'd have time with his brother.

Zak had almost immediately become infatuated with Paulette, despite her being great with child by another man, and Grant had feared the entire trip would be for nothing. He'd fumed and fussed to no avail as Zak continued to pursue his futile search and his obsession with the blond beauty.

Then after only a few weeks in the small Tennessee town, after meeting the lovely Tara, after the Halloween costume party, only then did Grant's headaches cease and he felt more like himself. When he'd gone home to see his specialists to set a course of treatment, they'd all been amazed at the clean images of his brain. No tumors. Anywhere. Somehow, something cured him, and he was determined to figure out what and how.

If only he knew where to begin his search.

If only the thought of Tara didn't prove wholly distracting.

He resumed his chore, muscles complaining at the extended workout. He lifted weights and jogged a couple of times a week to stay fit. But the effort required to dig and lift used different muscles. Perhaps he should get out into the field more often. He hadn't gone hiking in ages. Rather he'd spent much of his time trapped in the lab examining soils and rocks, analyzing field data but not collecting any himself. Hmph. Maybe he should do something about his confinement in the city office. Standing outside on such a pretty day happened less and less frequently. He missed being out in nature, the best aspect of his chosen profession.

As boys, he and Zak had spent hours outside, combing the area for unique rocks and outcroppings. Over time his knowledge of the mineral content of the soil based on the geologic formations and stratification made him highly respected in his field. He had plaques on his office wall as evidence of certain prestigious organizations' recognition of his abilities as both an analyst and geological consultant. Although, to be honest, consulting proved more difficult to get his foot in the door. Something he'd like to pursue now that he once again had a future ahead of him. His background and experience combined to make him uniquely qualified. He understood how anomalies of rocks and fossils occurred through transportation by animals and water. How human trade enabled the dispersion of various artifacts made from stone and quartz into areas where they didn't naturally occur. How layers of sediment developed and changed with heat and pressure over vast amounts of time. All of that knowledge didn't come from textbooks or journal articles. He needed to explore the outdoors more often to refresh and revitalize his passion for geology.

The plantation caretaker, Sean Williams, grunted as he swung the pickax to loosen the stump of a small nuisance tree cut down to enable other shade trees to be planted on either side of the winding path. The man had tended the property for decades, along with his wife, Meg. Together they had kept the place up and took care of the residents and the frequent bed and breakfast guests. Meg's cooking was renowned in the county with good reason. Just the thought of her chicken corn chowder and corn bread made his mouth water.

Sean swung again, and a pang of sadness at the loss of the mimosa surprised Grant as the man worked. The species was considered by landscapers as messy and thus not desirable, but he had a special fondness for the flowing pink blossoms. So delicate and yet resilient. Like a fine woman. Which made him think of Tara. Again. How she'd smelled of some delicate, flowery perfume when she'd gyrated closer and closer to him on the dance floor. The light touch of her fingers on the sides of his head, as brief and tantalizing as butterfly kisses. The sway of her hips and the lift of her breasts when after a minute or two she had smiled and sidled away, leaving behind the inexplicable desire to reach out and pull her to him. A move that would lead to trouble since they'd only met during the one week he spent in town and shared only polite conversation as he'd bought a coffee at the bookstore. She'd delighted him by shaking off the other party guests to dance with him instead. One dance had left him wanting more, even while knowing they were too different. Too set in their own career paths to compromise. Or at least that was true one month ago. His future appeared muddied and uncertain, undefined yet. Still, his mind refused to cooperate and think about something else. Or someone. He shoved the blade into the hard ground with more vigor.

"What's the matter?" Sean glanced at him, resting for a minute by leaning on the pickax handle, his blue-and-green plaid flannel shirt unbuttoned over a pale gray shirt and dark blue jeans.

"Nothing." Not that he'd share. It made no sense to be so infatuated with a woman he barely knew. "I'm just not used to yard work, I guess."

"You're doing fine." Sean hefted the pick. He spread his booted feet apart and prepared to swing the ax then paused and put the tool on the ground. "Looks like we've got some help. Hey, Zak."

Grant looked up to see his older brother approaching the construction site. Tall with dark hair graying at the temples, he looked content in a way he'd never been before he'd married Paulette a mere month ago. Even his stride, long and loose, demonstrated how relaxed and comfortable he was. By contrast, Grant couldn't sleep or focus. Except on the unnatural mesmerizing attraction he experienced for the temptress Tara and the mystery he needed to solve. Yet being back in Tennessee brought him a sense of happiness unlike any other place he'd been. His heart fairly sang at being in the small town near to his brother and Tara. Inexplicably Tara. Hell, he'd never even taken her on a date. One dance at the costume party barely counted. He couldn't stop thinking about her. Especially after sitting so close to her the other day in his car, and then trying not to stare at her when she sat across the table during dinner. He had to force himself to look away as she placed loaded chips into her mouth or embarrass himself at the dinner table. What the hell was wrong with him?

"Hey, Sean. Grant." Zak halted beside the cleared space and folded his arms. "Need some help?"

"If you want." Sean motioned to the wheelbarrow and the collection of tools it held. "We're laying the path out, winding like Meredith asked. Grab a shovel and start digging up the sod and put it in that wagon." He waved a hand toward the small work wagon hitched to the lawn tractor.

"Why don't you rent a Bobcat?" Zak moved to the barrow and lifted one handle and then another, finally retrieving a flat blade spade. "This would go a lot faster if you did."

The small bulldozer type tractor would scrape away the grass and top soil with more efficiency than men and shovels. Still, the fuel consumed and the smoke added to the atmosphere would leave its negative effect on the area. Grant appreciated the need for speed many people seemed to favor, but at the same time, he also understood how the mechanization adversely affected the land and air. A trade-off necessary to make depending on the desired result.

Besides, he enjoyed working with his hands to create something beautiful and lasting.

Meredith and Paulette lived on the family plantation along with their husbands, working to restore and repair the buildings after years of neglect and storm damage. Grant had witnessed the sisters working out whatever animosity they allowed to come between them until they reclaimed their friendship. Paulette had even persuaded Meredith not to destroy the manor but instead create a memory garden where others could plant a tree, bush, or whatever in honor of someone they loved and lost. A sanctuary where they could walk or sit and remember.

Sean shook his head and sighed. "The environmental impact would be much greater if we did that. Meredith and I agreed to do it with as little equipment as possible to lessen the damage to the ecosystem."

"Since when did you get all naturalist on us?" Zak chuckled as he started digging.

"Since Meredith said she wanted to create something lovely and meaningful that didn't destroy the property in the process." Sean lifted the pick and prepared to swing it again. "Sustainable, I think she called it."

Grant let his gaze trail across the meadow, landing on the historic manor house with its large sleeping porches overlooking the rear of the property. He could see the edge of the lake out front. The caretaker's cottage snuggled into the shade of several large maples not far from an inviting gazebo with cushioned chairs. Two magnolias flanked the gate to the family cemetery with its neatly arranged tombstones, yet another fix Sean had made to the property since Grant's last visit. Adding in a memorial garden would attract more visitors to the property and ensure it remained a place of love and peace for the foreseeable future.

"We need to assess the impact to the water table and the lake as well." Grant chopped another section of turf and scooped it into the wagon. "I'm sure Meredith probably considered contacting the Corps of Engineers for their assistance."

"She incorporated their study feedback into the layout to prevent any problems." Sean fingered the wooden handle of the pickax and then held it across his torso. "As long as we follow her plan, we'll be fine."

"Whatever makes my sister-in-law happy makes me happy." Zak placed a booted foot on the top of the spade blade and stomped down. He repeated the process to cut out a square of the sod and then flung it onto the nearby wagon.

"Is it always this warm in late November?" Grant kept his hand busy with the shovel, digging up ground covering vines by the roots and adding them to the growing pile. "It's almost Thanksgiving and still in the 70s."

"Not always, but I'll take it." Zak stuck the spade in the earth again and dug up a clump of grass. Grabbing the green blades, he shook off the dirt and then tossed the clump into the growing pile. "Speaking of Thanksgiving, you're invited to join us for dinner at the Golden sisters' house, since you'll still be in town."

Dinner with Tara? What a great idea. A wave of pleasure coursed through him as her face appeared in his mind's eye. Her pretty brown hair with blond highlights glinting in the sunshine. Serious hazel eyes nestled among thick dark lashes. The way she'd graciously handled the taco shell fire in the kitchen, resorting to humor and not to tears or tantrums. The idea of being with her for the upcoming holiday made his heart swell. But he didn't want to wait so long. He needed a plan. "Sounds good. Besides, there's a certain brunette I've had my eye on."

"Aha. I thought a woman must be involved to keep you away from your dirt and rocks and gems." Zak stabbed the blade into the ground and continued his task, slowly inching across the width of the planned trail. "Is it Tara? You two seemed to hit it off at the party."

"She's hot." She drew him to her like iron to a lodestone. Grant added more clumps of turf to the wagon, making the pile precariously high, and then leaned on the wooden handle of the shovel. "What if I were to start seeing her? Would that be insane or what?"

"Seriously?" Zak halted in the middle of aiming for another cluster of blades. "From up north?"

"I don't know. It's just a whim. Probably not a good idea at that." Could he manage a long-distance relationship with a certain lady? He mentally shook himself. He was thinking crazy thoughts.

"Not a bad one." Zak emptied his shovel into the nearly overflowing wagon. "You know you're welcome to stay with us as often as you'd like, right? So you could visit her."

"Never mind. Ignore my dumb idea." Grant's gut clenched at the realization. The thought of only seeing her on infrequent visits. He shook off the disappointment flooding his soul and pointed to the wagon near to overflowing with their efforts. "How about if I trundle that wagon of sod to a dumping place?"

Sean paused in pulling the stump up. "Give me a hand with this and then take it all over to the pile by the fence. I'll use it to fill in some holes around the place."

"What kind of holes?" Grant tossed his spade into the wheelbarrow before walking over to stand by Sean. "Nothing too big?"

"A few depressions, ones I'm hoping don't become sink holes like those that opened up outside Winchester recently." Sean propped his pickax against the wheelbarrow and dusted off his gloved hands.

"Those things are unpredictable at the best of times." Grant moved to the other side of the stump from Sean. "Some hint or clue they'll form, maybe, if you know what to look out for, but often it's too late by the time you know what you're dealing with."

"Let's hope I'm wrong then." Sean grinned at Grant, including Zak in his happy countenance. "Ready?"

"If you are." Grant stepped closer and bent to get a grip.

Zak shifted to move farther away. "I'll stand over here if you all don't mind."

Grant and Sean grabbed hold of the loosened stump and together pulled it out of the ground. Shaking off the roots first, Sean heaved it on top of the turf pile. Grant strode over to start the tractor and drive it slowly across the meadow to the location indicated. While he shoveled the contents onto the ground, his thoughts stayed on Tara. On what he suspected was a mutual attraction between them. On the distance between them, both in miles and willingness to be together. How might he satisfy both his obligations and his desires? Finishing his task, he closed the rear tailgate and then drove to position the wagon for the next load. Shutting off the engine, he grabbed his shovel from the bed and continued the job.

After several minutes he caught his brother's eye. "I suppose I should get to know Tara better before I make such a rash decision?" Grant shook his head and studied Zak for several moments. "Maybe ask her out?"

Zak guffawed as he resumed his work. "That's probably a good starting point."

"I thought so." He grinned in return and focused on the task at hand. Monday morning he'd stop in the bookstore and see if she agreed.

Chapter Eight

"Where is it?" Tara scanned the shelf of cookbooks in the pantry. Maybe if she could find the right book. The one her mom had used most often. Trailing a finger along each worn cover, she tried to recall which one might help her with desserts. Easy desserts. Ones she could make that would taste good.

Frustrated, she grabbed several of them, juggling them in her arms as she stepped out of the closet and then stacked them on the table. Repeating the process three more times, she finally had all of them precariously stacked in plain view. Standing back to glare at the piles, her heart thudded against her ribcage. Fear of failure ricocheted in her mind, paralyzing her as she dragged in air to try to calm herself. Sundays were meant for relaxing and meditation, not anxiously searching for answers. She could continue tomorrow, ignore the pressing need to make a decision for one more day. Roxie's disappointed expression floated through her thoughts. Rekindled the dismay she'd experienced. Tara cleared her throat and straightened her shoulders. She'd find a way not to let her sister down. Not to let the family down.

Sliding out the chair, she settled onto it and picked the

first book off the nearest stack. Opening it, she scanned the table of contents. All she saw were elaborate sounding endeavors that quailed her determination. She closed the book and set it aside, pulling another off the pile and opening it. Flipped through the contents and then slammed it shut. Surely one of the books would hold something she could manage. She repeated the process, growing more confused and less confident with each passing minute. When she'd gone through all of them with no better idea of what to choose, she propped her head on her hands, elbows on the checked table cloth, and closed her eyes.

Think. Where might she find contenders for Thanksgiving dessert? While the books held lots of possibilities, deciding on which ones proved elusive. She needed to narrow her options. If only she could employ Boolean operators on the index… That was the answer. She raised her head and pushed away from the table. Hurrying to her purse, she pulled out her phone and quickly typed in the search criteria: easy dessert recipes. Within moments a long list of links appeared and she began skimming the plethora of ideas. An overwhelming number of ideas. Mind-blowing, really. So much for weeding out those too complex or challenging. As she read through the links, the very titles seemed to suggest complicated recipes.

Frozen Raspberry Pistachio Terrine? Hmmm, what exactly was terrine? If she didn't know what the thing was, then it was probably best to keep looking. Raspberry Truffles? No way. Ice Cream Cake? That might be a possibility. Then again, why not just serve ice cream? But frozen wasn't baking. She sighed. The list contained dozens of cookie recipes, which wouldn't suit the need. Her need to prove to her sister, and to herself, that she could prepare a delectable after-dinner treat or two. She kept searching as footsteps sounded in the hallway.

Beth came into the kitchen and then stopped, drawing Tara's attention away from the device in her hands. Beth's jaw slowly dropped open as her brows raised over wide eyes. "What on earth are you doing?"

Tara noted the surprise and hint of alarm in her sister's eyes. "Trying to decide what to make for dessert. What's it look like?"

"Like you've lost your ever-loving mind." Shaking her head slowly, Beth continued across the room to stand beside Tara. Peering over her shoulder, she laughed. "Wow. Who knew there were so many possibilities."

Too many. Tara perused the stacks before her with the absolute knowledge she would fail. Fantastically, no doubt. She who couldn't even warm sticky buns in the oven without issues. She pressed her eyes closed for two seconds and then opened them to regard her sister.

"It's mind-boggling." Tara tossed her phone onto the table and sighed. "I just don't know what to do. Thanksgiving is only four days away, and I have no clue."

Beth studied her, tapping one hand on her crossed arms. "You're overreacting."

"How so?"

"I could help you."

"Would you?" Hope blossomed in the pit of Tara's stomach like the first notes of a song.

"You're my sister. I can tell you're concerned so of course I'll help you."

But what about Beth's other cooking responsibilities? It wasn't fair to ask her to do more. Besides, Roxie had placed her faith in Tara. She believed Tara possessed the ability to make dessert. A seemingly simple task. Asking for help would only reinforce Roxie's belief that Tara couldn't push past her mental barrier. She had to succeed on her terms or not at all.

"Thanks but no." Tara sighed as she rubbed a finger on

the side of her nose to relieve an itch. "I need to do this myself."

"Roxie didn't say you couldn't ask for help." Beth grinned. "Maybe your reluctance is not about needing help. Maybe it's more than that. Are you by chance worried about having Grant here? I mean, I think he's cute and all, so if you don't want him…"

"Why does everyone think there's something between us? I barely know the man. He paid more attention to you than me at dinner the other night." One dance at a party didn't mean they were an item. Even if she found herself reliving the minutes they'd spent together like a never-ending film loop. Proving her body did not always agree with her head. "Besides, you know what happened the last time a guy found out about my powers." Tara shook her head as she plopped onto the chair.

She had thought Ned had potential. He'd asked her out while she was studying at the local college, and for five glorious weeks, she had been in love. They were inseparable, attending the monthly dances, going to the movies, taking long walks through the country, and simply hanging out on the square. She blithely assumed he cared for her. All of her and her capabilities. Until the day when he'd tripped and fallen while they were biking along a winding lane outside of town. His cry of pain when he tried to break his fall alerted her to his broken wrist. Without considering the consequences, she wrapped both hands around the joint. When she let go, Ned stared at her, breathing faster and faster, eyes widening in alarm.

She'd tried to calm him, to explain, but when she said the word "witch," he'd popped to his feet and took off running for his bike. He never talked to her again, always steering clear of her whenever he saw her approaching. He never told anyone about her powers as far as she could determine. Probably afraid he'd be called crazy for his efforts. The ordeal taught her a very hard lesson, never to reveal her abilities to anyone. She'd kept her vow to protect her heart from such pain and devastation. She'd built a shield of defense tough enough to prevent anyone from breaking through. Until Grant showed up.

"Ouch. I do. But Grant seems different." Beth reached to pick up the *Joy of Baking* from among the mess of books on the table. She opened it, almost reverently she turned the pages one by one. "This was Mom's favorite."

Tara peered at the page where Beth had paused. Banana nut bread caught her eye. "Remember when Mom would make that?"

Beth drew a finger down the page, pausing at the few ingredients listed. "She could make the best around. Did Mom ever tell you her secret ingredient?"

Tara aimed raised brows up at her sister. Her hope shattered into splinters. "Secret ingredient?"

Beth slowly closed the book and placed it back on the haphazard pile. "She didn't tell me what it was, but she always put something in that's not listed in the book."

"I'm doomed." Tara slapped her hands against her forehead and rested her heavy head on her palms. "I can't measure up no matter what I do."

Beth chuckled and tapped Tara on the shoulder. Tara lifted her head to gaze at her sister, letting her hands fall into her lap. Beth shook her head as she tugged on Tara's arm until she stood.

Beth pulled Tara around to look at her. After a moment, she dropped her hands to her sides. "First, you need to get a grip on reality."

"What reality?" Tara stared at Beth, waiting. Would she have some insight Tara had missed?

"It's not a contest. You're not going to be judged on the outcome."

"Sure I am. Roxie will be assessing whether I've succeeded or failed yet again." Tara crossed her arms, wrapping them around herself like a protective blanket. "I don't want to let her down. Or the family for that matter. This is too important."

If the dinner were only for the three sisters, then Tara wouldn't worry quite so much. Adding in the two cousins and their husbands, and then Grant as the cherry on top created havoc in her stomach. His opinion mattered more to her than it probably should, given how little she knew about him. Beth had expressed interest in him and Tara had high hopes they would become a couple. Leaving her to quell her own feelings. Despite the knowledge she and Grant shared an attraction on the molecular level. But a repellant on a logical level as far as where he lived and worked and what he'd say about her being a witch. The resulting disconnect put her heart in peril. She mentally reinforced the shield, hoping it proved strong enough to protect her.

Beth shook her head, crossing her arms over her chest. "You don't get it."

Tara studied Beth's face, seeing the sincerity in her steady gaze. Love and concern blending to soften her features as she contemplated Tara. "What don't I get?"

The middle sister had been the glue holding the three of them together since the loss of their mother. Her compassion and consistency enabled her to not only accurately understand any situation, any personality, and any clash of wills, but also to see ways to steer the people toward a better situation or resolution. Almost as if she could see into the future. Which of course she could. Maybe Tara should listen more closely to what she had to say.

"Roxie won't judge you harshly. She only wants us to work together to share a tradition in our family with our newest additions."

"I feel like she wants to show us off to them or something." Tara hugged herself tighter.

"It's her way of welcoming them. More to the point, the three of us will work together to create a holiday meal and a new tradition." Beth laid her hands on Tara's upper arms and slowly slid her hands down to prompt Tara to unwrap her arms. Eventually, Beth held both of Tara's hands in hers as she leaned closer to emphasize her next words. "It's *not* a trial."

"It feels like a test. And you know how much I hate exams."

Beth squeezed Tara's hands briefly and then released them. "I know, which is why I'm trying to tell you that you need to relax and make something you will enjoy sharing with the rest of us."

"No pressure, huh?" Tara turned to the stacks of cookbooks. Not only would she let down her family, but she'd also embarrass herself in front of Grant. An event she'd do anything to avoid. *Anything*. "If I could believe that, perhaps this would be easier."

Chapter Nine

A group of school-aged children rode their bikes through the town square. Grant parked his car near the Golden Owl Books and Brews. Shoppers and tourists with their cameras at the ready crowded the sidewalks. With the holiday season beginning, more people had descended on the quaint town to buy gifts, gather at the many restaurants, or shop in the boutiques. The bookstore also drew shoppers, as Grant discovered when he entered the bustling business.

He hesitated inside the door, the tiny bell announcing his entrance jangling into silence above him. Nerves simmered in his stomach, roiling his quick breakfast into a painful knot. Scanning the room, he nodded to Roxie and then espied Beth behind the coffee counter waiting on customers. Where was Tara?

Strolling farther into the store, he made his way past the displays of jewelry and stationary toward the shelves and shelves of books. As he passed the door to the workroom, he peeked inside. Empty. He let his gaze drift over the expanse before him but still did not see the woman he sought. Glancing up at the second floor, he decided to climb the stairs to see if she might be among the nonfiction books.

When he reached the top, he perused the sections slowly until he spotted her. Head bent over an array of colorful covers.

Taking a moment to observe her, he lingered at the edge of the large balcony crammed with chest-high shelves of books surrounding a group of tables and chairs. Leaning against the railing, he watched her. The carpeted path from where he stood to the wooden table where she worked provided a direct line of sight of her pretty features marred by a frown of concentration. Long hair pulled up into a neat ponytail draped over her left shoulder. He could gaze on her beauty as long as she'd let him. Longer. Trim but not skinny. Pretty but not vain. Smart and funny to boot. She might not be perfect, but she was damn close.

She chewed on a pencil for several moments and then jotted notes on a pad of paper at her right. Her intensity surprised him. What was she doing? Surrounded by so many books while she was supposed to be working. The sight didn't bode well. Perhaps he could help her. He couldn't figure out her objective from afar, so he pushed off the railing.

He strode to where she intently pored over a large book with colored pictures of nut pies evident. Must be getting ready for the dinner in a few days. His mouth watered at the sight of the pecan and walnut pies. Thanksgiving couldn't come soon enough. "Howdy." He jumped when she startled at the sound of his voice. "Whoa, sorry. I didn't mean to scare you."

Tara placed a hand at her throat and shook her head as she gazed up at him. "My bad. I wasn't paying attention."

"What are you doing?" He leaned closer to peer at the page. "Pecan pie with honey and maple syrup? Sounds good."

She gave a long, heartfelt release of pent up air, and dropped the pencil on the pad. "And complicated."

"It's easy as pie, right?" He chuckled at his joke only to stop at the glare Tara aimed at him. "What's wrong?"

"Nothing. I'll figure it out." She glanced over the mess of books and then stood and started stacking them in preparation for shelving them. "What brings you in today?"

"You, actually." Did he just blurt that out? What was wrong with him? "I mean—"

She grabbed several of the books, fumbling them into a bundle in her arms, and brushed past him. "I've got work to do, so if you'll excuse me."

He followed her, grasping for the right words. How did one ask a beautiful woman on a date without making a fool of himself in the process? He'd already bungled it with his outburst. As she placed the last book in her arms on the shelf, he stepped in front of her. Blocking her retreat to the table for another group of cookbooks.

"Tara, please." Should he take her hands? No, probably not. He rubbed one hand across his nape. "Spare me a few minutes?"

She crossed her arms and studied him, blinking slowly. "Very well. What do you want?"

"I'd like to take you out on a date." He inched closer, reducing the escape route as he pressed his case. "I cannot stop thinking of our dance together."

"Dance?" Her voice emerged breathy and hesitant.

"At the costume party." Surely she remembered. He hoped. "At Twin Oaks."

She bobbed her head twice. "Right."

"Will you go out with me?" Please say yes. He waited for her response, holding his breath until he had to inhale or die.

She opened her mouth to say something only to be interrupted by Beth approaching. Blast. Talk about timing. Bad timing. Grant greeted Beth with a nod.

"What brings you in today?" Beth smiled at him, eager to chat.

"I came to ask Tara out." He liked Beth because she was direct and yet didn't make him uncomfortable. He shot a sideways glance at Tara and then returned Beth's smile. "She's keeping me in suspense."

"Say yes, Tara." Beth nodded at Tara, sneaking a quick peek at Grant before leveling her gaze on her sister. She widened her eyes as she studied her. "You need a break."

Tara shook her head as a slight frown formed between her eyes. "I've got too much to do. I can't."

What would entice Tara to accept his invitation despite her workload? A cup of coffee? A movie?

"Everyone needs to play occasionally." Beth shook a finger at Tara, a smile on her face. "You don't want to become dull, right?"

"It's my day to organize the stationery and jewelry displays." Tara folded her arms, a protective wall shutting Grant out. "Before we have too many customers pawing through them on Black Friday."

"You've plenty of time to do that later." Beth included Grant in her glance. "Listen to me. Accept his offer and go out with him."

Tara slid her gaze to Grant, and he smiled at her. Encouraging her with every fiber of his being. He needed her to follow her sister's advice.

"Why don't you go and I'll get my work done?" Tara's expression revealed a hint of desperation.

Beth raised a brow and shook her head. "He asked you, not me."

"Please?" Grant sidled closer, hoping to influence her decision. "I promise you'll have a good time."

"And do what?" Tara regarded Grant for a moment, then glanced between him and her sister. "There's not much to do in Roseville."

Encouraged by her question, Grant ran through the obvious choices. "We could grab a coffee."

Tara tossed her hair with an exasperated jerk of her head. "We serve that here."

"A movie?" Grant dredged his memory for what was playing at the two-screen cinema in town. "I think there's a horror flick playing."

"Horror?" She shook her head, sending Beth a pleading glance. "Not my thing. See, there's nothing to do in town."

"What about outside of town?" Grant scrambled to think of another option. Then an idea popped into his brain. "How about a hike in the woods?"

"A hike?"

"You could take a picnic and make a day of it." Beth grinned and tapped Tara on the shoulder. "Sounds like a fun kind of date."

Hope and victory fought inside Grant as he watched Tara contemplate the idea. He didn't know if she liked to be out in nature, but if so that was a happy coincidence on his part. Also a good match for their chances of finding common ground on which to build a relationship. If only she'd say yes.

Tara tilted her head to one side as she shook it. "It's tempting, but no. I really must stay and focus on what I need to get done. Perhaps another time, Grant."

She made to push past Beth but was stopped by that woman's hand on her upper arm. They exchanged a long look, complete with raised and lowered eyebrows and tilts of their head. Beth made a moue and pressed her palms together as if praying. Tara sighed and dropped her shoulders before turning to Grant. Their silent debate showed how close the sisters were to each other. And that Beth was on his side.

"Fine. When and where?"

Victory won the battle in Grant's chest. "Awesome. Tomorrow morning? I hear there's a state park about thirty miles from here that has some cool geological sites worth checking out."

Tara laced her fingers together in front of her waist and shifted her weight to her left hip. "I'll pack the picnic if you don't mind store-bought deli."

"I'll bring the rest of the gear." Grant mentally categorized the tools he'd bring for extracting small soil or rock samples as well as survival necessities. He never went hiking without taking the proper precautions. Not since the tragedy he'd caused as a boy. No way would he let another person come to harm as a result of his actions. "The weather is supposed to remain mild until Thanksgiving, so dress in layers."

"What gear do you need?" Tara aimed puzzled eyes at him. "It's just a hike."

He smiled if a bit grimly. Nature could turn on a hiker without warning. Best to be prepared for any occasion. But he didn't want to cause her alarm, so he kept those thoughts to himself. "I don't go out in the field without being prepared. You never know what we might find. Expect the unexpected, in other words, and hope you're right that it's just a simple hike."

"You have doubts?" Tara regarded him with a hint of concern reflected in her eyes.

"Always." He softened his expression to relieve her worry. "I'll be there to take care of you, Tara. Have no doubt on that score."

Chapter Ten

She'd never played hooky from work before as the tension in her stomach proved. Tara opened the passenger door of Grant's car and eased out of the vehicle. Grabbing the picnic backpack from the floor of the car, she hefted it onto her shoulders. The morning sunshine warmed her face as she watched wispy clouds drifting across a pale sky. Then focused on the surrounding hills covered with forest as far as she could see. Grant had said he'd take her away from town, away from the hustle and bustle of her day-to-day life, but this wilderness was more than she'd bargained for. What critters lurked among the trees? What if an escaped convict hid in those hills? She shaded her eyes with one hand, her imagination taking flight and stirring up a bevy of most likely silly scenarios as she scanned the area. Then she glanced at her companion and her stomach flipped over.

Grant had that effect on her. His presence, his evident strength, and confidence enveloped her like a bear hug even as her heart raced and her insides melted. A warm comfort, like returning home after a long trip, charming her like nobody had ever done before. The reason why she couldn't refuse his invitation despite her reluctance. Beth's prompting pushed her the way she wanted to go but had resisted. She must protect herself. Time with Grant could set her up for a broken heart when he left. Which she knew he fully intended to do after Thanksgiving. For now, she'd guard her heart as best she could and enjoy the day with sexy, handsome Grant. The time with him would give her more opportunity to nudge him in Beth's direction. A grin lifted the corners of her mouth. A day with a hunky guy to persuade him to date her sister. She could do that. After all, what could it hurt to try?

She zipped her light jacket, glad she'd finally settled on a flowered pullover sweater, blue jeans, and sturdy tennis shoes. The breeze remained cool this early in the day, lifting and shifting her hair as it hung around her shoulders, a few stray strands hooking on her lip. She slipped a band from her wrist and pulled her hair into a ponytail to end the annoyance. She dropped her hands when she noticed Grant watching her, his mouth open.

"What?" Had he been staring at her chest while she'd done up her hair? Or something else? "What's wrong?"

Slowly the dazed expression morphed into his normal easy grin. "Nothing. Might as well leave your phone in the car." Grant gazed at her over the roof of the white car for several seconds as he adjusted his backpack on his shoulders. He dropped a hand out of sight and then waggled his phone at her before tossing it onto the seat and closing the door. "Not only won't we need them, but there's no service this far from town."

"I don't go anywhere without it." The very idea sent a shaft of alarm into her stomach, as if she'd stepped outside naked. She fingered the device in her jeans pocket as she stared at Grant over the expanse of roof. "I can't leave it behind."

"Just turn it off and drop it inside. You'll be fine without it. Trust me." He winked at her, key fob in hand ready to lock the car after she complied with his suggestion.

The phone provided more than a means to call someone. Once, she'd only used it to make calls, but now the device enabled so many other functions. Maps and directions. Internet access to search on whatever she needed to know. Games and puzzles as a distraction. But most important, her camera. Grant waited, a quirked brow the only indication of any hint of impatience.

"Live in the moment, Tara. You don't need your phone while we're out wandering the woods together."

"You just don't want yours so that you're not distracted from my beauty, is that it?" She grinned at him, relaxing as she enjoyed the feeling of playing hooky from work with the handsome man she couldn't resist. He had a point about enjoying the experience without seeing it through the lens of her camera. She threw her phone on the seat and closed her door. "Fine. I'll trust you, but you better not let me down."

"You'll be safe with me. Never fear." Grant pressed the button and shoved the keys into a zipped pocket on his backpack. "Let's go. This place promises to be amazing."

"I've never been this far out in the woods before." She fell in beside him as they crossed the parking lot and took the first steps on the trail into the forest. "How did you find it?"

"I've heard about the Cumberland Plateau from some coworkers for a long time and wanted to explore it but never had the chance until now." He held a branch aside until she passed and then released it. "It has quite a history."

"Of bootlegging and rum runners, right?" She chuckled as she trudged along, searching the underbrush and trees for movement of wildlife. "They could certainly have hidden out here for a long time with no one finding them."

Grant huffed a laugh as he held out a hand to help her over a fallen tree on the path. She placed her fingers in his, startled by the buzz of awareness traveling up her arm straight to her heart. She inhaled sharply, detected pine and earth and his spicy cologne. Stepping over the obstacle, she stopped in front of him.

"Thanks." She searched his expression and found a sparkle of interest in his eyes. Her fingers tingled from their prolonged contact. Her grand intentions blew away on the slight breeze. He had to touch her, didn't he? The one act capable of demolishing her resistance.

"My pleasure." His expression grew serious as he gazed at her. He lifted her unresisting hand to press a kiss to her palm. "I'm glad you came with me today."

She nodded, speech not possible for several moments. "You forced me into it."

He kept her hand in his and started walking again. The strength of his grip satisfied a longing she tried to deny but couldn't. It felt so right she let him retain his hold on her even though she ought to stop him. Ought to pull away and say something about Beth. But she couldn't force the action or the words. He helped her up a steep incline until the trail leveled off and followed a ridge for several hundred feet. Birds flitted through the trees, singing to each other. A rustle in the bushes startled her and Grant squeezed her hand. She peeked at him, saw him smile encouragingly at her. She squeezed his hand back and they continued on their way.

"Are you glad to leave behind whatever was bothering you yesterday to come out and experience nature at its best?"

"You had to remind me." Not that she'd forgotten. Not by a long shot. Even the distraction of his strong fingers wrapped around hers couldn't dislodge the gauntlet she'd picked up.

"What's upsetting you?" Grant glanced at her and then looked ahead to navigate the leaf-littered trail.

Between the impending dessert disaster and her inability to resist Grant, how could she choose only one thing? "I'll take care of it when we get back." She inhaled and let the breath out slowly. "It's something I need to handle myself."

They walked in silence for several moments, each lost in their own thoughts. A black bird winged across the path and landed in a tree. A second followed and perched on a nearby branch. A couple of pretty big birds with dark purple, iridescent wings and a hooked bill. Could they be ravens? She shivered as mythical tales of horror and death associated with them filled her head. Their dark plumage had frequently been judged an ill omen, a very bad sign. Great. Like she needed another sign. They seemed to follow her progress down the trail, croaking to each other in short bursts of sound, before flying away. She rolled her shoulders to ease the burning tension in them.

She flicked a glance at Grant. "Where are we going? You haven't told me that."

"This trail will take us to the state forest that spans the county line. I understand there are some particularly spectacular geologic sites worth seeing." He brushed a spider's web to one side to allow her to pass and then fell into step beside her. "Some of the cliffs date back eons, to the Pennsylvanian geologic period. I'd love to see that as well as the beautiful sandstones and shale."

"Is that why you've brought a backpack of stuff?" She motioned to the bulging bag of mysterious items on his back. "To do some digging or something?"

"Not in the state forest, that's protected land. But outside of it maybe. Basically, I don't go hiking without being prepared for anything."

"So what's in it?" His voice sent goosebumps down her arms. She wanted him to keep talking.

"My tools, protein bars, bottled water, flashlight, compass, a thirty-foot rope, and of course a first-aid kit. The essentials."

"Were you a Boy Scout?" She glanced at him in time to catch a flash of pain crossing his face. "What's wrong?"

"I learned as a boy to never take chances." He dropped her hand as the trail narrowed and he took the lead.

She sensed his withdrawal as he'd mentioned his childhood, felt a distance between them having nothing to do with the size of the path they traversed. Then he glanced at her over his shoulder and smiled, warming the air and closing the emotional distance at the same time. She mentally shook her head, pushing away the odd sensation. When the trail opened up again, he extended a hand and waited. She shouldn't, but the compulsion to touch him won. She gave him her hand and they continued deeper and deeper into the forest.

"Did you know that this area is known for having the highest concentration of underground caves in the country?" Grant glanced at her and then let his gaze drift away to examine their surroundings.

"No, I didn't."

"It's why the National Speleological Society moved its headquarters to Huntsville, Alabama, the closest relatively large city." Grant swept an arm to encompass the hills stretching away before them. "Beneath most of this land are countless caverns and caves just waiting for spelunkers to discover and explore. I go caving every chance I have."

Tara chuckled at the enthusiasm in his deep voice. "Wow, you do like caves and such, don't you?"

"Yes. They provide a glimpse into the underbelly of our planet and what it's made of. I'm intrigued by how life exists even in the darkest recesses. You know, where light doesn't reach from outside."

"I hate the dark. I wouldn't want to be stuck in a cave without being able to see what was around me. Ever." She shuddered at the thought of having no way to tell what might lurk around her, waiting to attack or press its advantage over the blind woman she'd become. Although the thought of being alone in the dark with Grant, now that was sigh worthy.

Grant lifted her hand to chest height and tugged her closer. "You needn't fear. I'll protect you from harm."

"From the dark?"

"I have a flashlight with which to defend you." He smiled at her as he lowered their joined hands. "We do not need to venture into any caves today if you'd rather not."

"We should find a spot to enjoy lunch before long. My tummy is growling."

"I'll keep an eye out for one. I'm starting to get hungry as well. Let's pick up the pace a bit."

The trail wound through the sun-dappled trees, slanting up and up as they walked along holding hands. She tried not to feel guilty for being too weak to pull away. She drank in the beauty of the woods, the sky peeking through the leafy trees, and kept her eyes open to spot any animals they might roust as they passed. Once or twice she thought she saw the pair of ravens but dismissed such a recurrence as unlikely.

Grant uttered a sound, half gasp and half laugh, and then pulled her off the marked trail to an overlook of the valley below. "Isn't that astounding?"

She followed his pointing finger to gaze upon the undulating hills covered in varying shades of green, gray, and brown as they marched away from beneath where they stood. She shaded her eyes to see the details more clearly. Suddenly, Grant squeezed her hand and then pulled her around to look up at him.

"Tara, would you let me kiss you?" He reached to grasp her other hand, drawing them both together as he urged her to move closer to him. His gaze flitted between her eyes and her mouth as the distance diminished. "I can't resist you."

All thought of anything other than the man begging her to kiss him fled her befuddled brain. The vital attraction she'd attempted to push aside claimed every shred of her being. She let him draw her in, anticipation and longing buzzing inside. She moistened her lips, Grant's eyes zeroing in on the movement like a hawk on a scampering field mouse. Caution flew to the winds the closer he came to kissing her.

He leaned in to press his lips to hers, and she lifted her mouth to meet his; shock ricocheting through her at the sensation flooding into her core. Being the meal had its benefits. Grant devoured her, his hands releasing hers to embrace her in a bear hug unlike any she'd experienced before. After several delirious moments, he eased away, gasping for air as if he'd run uphill. She understood the need for air after being blown apart by his kiss. She opened her mouth to say something—what, she didn't know—when the ground beneath them trembled.

She clutched hold of his hands, eyes flying open. The air shimmered around them. The birds stopped singing. She spied the pair of ravens flying overhead, seeming to look down on her and then dip their wings as if waving. Odd. Indeed all was still around them for a heartbeat. Grant grabbed her as the earth shook again and then plummeted away. Tara screamed as they fell into a hole that widened rapidly and deepened into darkness. Panic sharp and piercing filled her. She gasped and clutched but couldn't gain purchase on the seeming slow-motion cascade of dirt and rocks. Earth and underbrush descended beneath them until they finally hit bottom with a gasp and a grunt. They tumbled to a halt after what seemed minutes of free fall.

"Grant! Where are you?" She scrambled onto her knees and reached out with both hands in the inky blackness. She had to remain calm. To think. Find Grant. Find light. Lifting her gaze to look up at where they'd fallen, she could dimly detect sunlight a very long ways above her. Lowering her gaze, she tried to see into the blackness. No shades of gray to discern. Searching the dark proved futile. Fear crawled up her throat. "Grant!"

"I'm here."

"I'm afraid! Where are you?" Splaying her hands she swept the area in front of her, searching for him. The isolating darkness awoke the terror from her childhood. Her heart raced in her chest, her breathing fast and shallow. Memories overlaid each other in her mind of falling into a dark, damp cellar and hitting her head as she tumbled to the bottom. Awaking in the hospital, her mother frantic at her bedside. Falling and darkness combined into panic she couldn't deny or dismiss. "Grant?"

"Calm down. Just a minute." Grant's movements sounded from her left, and then a light appeared. "Are you all right?"

She sighed shakily as she ran her hands over her arms and legs. "I think so." Hearing his voice stemmed the rising tide of panic. She squinted into the welcome beam of his flashlight. "Can you point that somewhere else?"

"I'm checking you out." The light played across her torn and dirty jacket then down to her dusty jeans. "I don't see any blood at least."

"Oh, I thought you meant you were *checking me out*." She chuckled humorlessly as the light continued its search down her legs to her shoes.

"I'm doing that inspection as well." His voice contained a smile as he diverted the path of the light to scan his feet and then his legs.

Tara saw only dirt and dust and thankfully no blood. She began to relax a tad. "Where are we? What happened?"

"I can't explain it. Somehow a sinkhole appeared where there shouldn't be one." The beam of light shook with his movements. "We were safely standing on what seemed to be packed ground. I don't understand."

Oh. She had an idea of what might have happened to them.

The shimmer of the air. The unexplained tremble in the earth. Had the ravens brought yet another bad omen? Or caused the hole to develop? It shouldn't be but there was no other explanation. But why? And by whom? Those questions she needed to find answers for. But in the meantime, one thing she knew for sure. "Magically?"

"No such thing as magic. It looks like the ceiling of a cave collapsed in for some reason. I can tell we're in some large underground room at least." Grant huffed, and the light bobbed away to flick around. Globs of dirt and stones tumbled down the sides of the pit, rolling to halt around them. "We can't stay here. It's still unstable. I can see a glimmer of light on the other side of this mound of dirt and such, which is probably where the original cave entrance was. But I can also see that there's a tunnel or something over there." The light aimed past her to the other side of the pit.

"Is it a way out?" She peered behind her and then glanced at the flashlight and dim outline of Grant.

"I hope so. Let's go see what we find." He took her hand to help her rise and they headed toward the opening. Grant continued to sweep the light from side to side as they cautiously eased into the dark tunnel. "Look."

The light lingered on a collection of wooden crates, burlap sacks, and a pair of wooden barrels, all of which had seen better days. Tara coughed as they stirred up dust when they stopped by the pile of boxes. The sacks were labeled as corn and grain, but lay torn to pieces by some long-gone scavenging animals. She hoped they were long gone anyway.

"Why is it so dusty in here?" Tara coughed again, one hand clutching Grant's shirt sleeve. "The collapse of the ground?"

Grant flicked the light around the medium-sized cave room and then back at her. "Given that somebody stored stuff here, I'd say the air here stayed dry so they could stash things for safe keeping."

"I'd heard that the soldiers in the Civil War used caves to store provisions and weapons." She glanced at the stack of wooden crates, the slats at various angles as they slowly disintegrated over time.

"You sound like you're skeptical."

"It seemed unlikely." Yet the evidence rested on the ground at her feet. "What's in those crates?"

Grant dropped her hand to open the top box, carefully lifting the lid and setting it aside. Tara peered around him into the interior illuminated by the pinpoint of light. Bundles wrapped in burlap sacks. Grant handed her the flashlight and reached inside to lift one out with both his hands. Carefully he unwrapped the object and then paused to examine it. Grease had been smeared on the metal of a gun. She stared in horror at the contents of the crate, calculating the number of weapons each might contain.

"Pistols." Grant wiped the grease off and then held the gun by the butt while he examined it. "Confederate. So the tales were true after all."

Tara stared at the weapon. She detested guns. The injuries they inflicted if they didn't kill. No matter if they were relics from a past national civil war. She didn't care if they were Confederate or Union. "Put it back."

Grant aimed the light closer to her and then away. "We may need it. If not to prove the rumors were not rumors, then to defend ourselves." He pried open the chamber and verified it was empty before slipping it into his belt. Then he reached into the box to remove a slim tan box with writing on top. She glimpsed the word "cartridges" before he opened the lid to check its contents. Neat rows of paper-wrapped black gunpowder cartridges waited to do their job.

Had waited a very long time and to her mind could continue to wait. Grant snapped the lid closed and slid the box into his pocket. "Just in case."

"Surely you won't need that." A simple hike had turned into something entirely more dangerous. On many, many levels. "Please."

"I hope I won't need to use it. We don't know where this tunnel will lead us and what we'll find. I promised to keep you safe, and that's what I'm going to do. Unlike... Never mind. Those guns have been buried here for a long, long time. Looks like they were packed well to preserve them for future use. But who knows whether it will fire or not. But if nothing else, it can be a club."

What if it misfired? She pushed the thought far from her mind. She'd not wish it on him. Tara wondered at his slight hesitation, what Grant had been about to say. But he obviously didn't want to share whatever had happened in the past to make him so protective. Perhaps one day he would feel comfortable sharing. But for now, he'd asked her to trust him, and that request was easy for her to follow because she had every reason to believe he could fulfill his promise.

Despite her reservations regarding the firearm, she took his hand and squeezed once. "I'll follow your lead, Grant."

He leaned closer to press a kiss on her mouth. "Let's find a way out of here."

Grant aimed the flashlight ahead of them, and they moved farther into the foreboding tunnel.

Chapter Eleven

*M*emories of that day long ago when his efforts in a similar situation had failed fought to the fore. Grant pushed them away but the dark tunnel seemed endless. The beam of light proved no match for the long, winding corridor he led Tara down. He hoped with each cautious turn to find even a glimmer of light ahead.

"Stay close." Grant placed each foot with care, testing for any weakness or obstacle before shifting his weight and repeating the process. His ability to see in near darkness gave him an advantage. He didn't know how well Tara could see so he kept her near to him. "Walk where I do."

"Can't you go a little faster?" Her grip on his hand tightened, the palm damp. "I hate being in the dark."

He wouldn't chance moving more quickly until the path became more visible. He couldn't risk a recurrence of his childhood failure and the resulting death. Not when he'd promised to protect Tara, that she'd be safe with him. He'd keep his promise without fail.

"Soon but not yet."

Tara squealed and pushed against his back when the scraping of unseen claws echoed around them. "What was that?"

"Just a rodent getting out of our way."

Her hand tugged on his as she shuddered. "Ugh. I want out of here."

He needed to keep her talking and with any luck maintain her present level of calm. "Why do you hate the dark so much?"

She sighed, clutching his hand in a death grip. "I've feared it ever since a child. When I fell down some cement steps into my parents' cellar."

Grant aimed the light along the rock-littered floor a little to the right, where he found the wall of the tunnel veering around yet another curve. At least she hadn't melted into a panic. Yet. "What happened?"

"I tripped chasing after one of my sisters while playing a game."

Walking carefully around the bend he kept the light dancing over the floor to steer Tara around the smattering of stones. "Were you badly hurt?"

"My mother found me unconscious at the bottom, blood pooled under my head. I woke up in the hospital." Tara inhaled sharply as more scrabbling echoed in front of them and then let the breath out slowly. "I had a slight concussion from hitting my head, and of course a cut. They bandaged me up and sent me home."

Swinging the flashlight to the left, Grant smothered a sigh of frustration. The tunnel fell away to the left and down. But down to where? "But why are you afraid of the dark?"

She gripped his hand until it ached. "The fear I felt when I fell into that dark and damp place has never left me. It was like being swallowed up by some monster of evil."

"Surely you don't believe in monsters. Watch your step here." He guided her around a larger flat rock and then down a step to a lower level.

Tara laughed for the first time since their sudden descent underground. "Not monsters, no."

Grant opened his mouth to ask her what she did believe in when the beam flickered. He jostled the handle, and the light strengthened. Although he didn't want to, he quickened their pace to attempt to reach some exit before the batteries died. If only he'd thought about spare ones he wouldn't worry about the one set giving out. He'd not expected they'd need a flashlight for long, if at all, since they had no intention of going caving. And yet there they were, walking along in the dark underground. The way leveled out and then turned right. When would the twists and turns end? He'd completely lost his sense of direction between the bends and the darkness. Once they found a way outside, he'd pull out the compass. But until then, they had to keep going. Keep moving. Not let fear take hold and thwart their escape from the hellhole they'd fallen into.

Like the well that his best friend Jeremy had fallen into when they were boys. He didn't let himself think about that day when he'd bragged about his navigational abilities. Back during a time he'd thought he could do anything when it came to hiking and climbing trees. Only he hadn't been able to prevent his friend from falling and breaking his back. From dying while Grant went for help.

Not again.

"We must be getting close to a way out." He'd stay positive for both of their sakes.

"Do you see a light ahead?"

"No, but we've been walking for quite a while." He slowed to a halt and turned the light to shine on Tara. "Do you need water?"

"Here?" Fear interlaced with the trust in her voice.

"Like I said, we've been walking for quite a while. We both need some. Hold this." He handed her the flashlight and then shrugged the backpack off his shoulders. Retrieving a bottle from a side pouch, he twisted open the lid and handed it to her.

She swallowed several mouthfuls before giving it back to him while maintaining the light so he could see. "When we find our way out of here, we still need to locate a place to eat our picnic, too."

Grant gulped twice and then replaced the lid before slipping the bottle into the pouch. He positioned the pack onto his shoulders, shrugging to settle the straps into place. "I'll take that light back."

"I should never have let you talk me into this nature outing. I'm more the town girl type." She offered it to him, and he wrapped his fingers around the barrel, awareness of her nearness pulsing through him. Enticing and tempting him to linger. "But now that you've got me out here, let's make the most of it and find a way out of this darkness."

"You've got it. Ready?"

"I was born ready…"

"Cute." He nodded and took her hand to keep her beside him as they continued on their quest for an exit. The floor sloped upward for a time, leveled off, and then curved to the left and back to the right. All the while he retained her hand and prayed the dimming light wouldn't fail. They eased around a bend to the left, and he almost cheered.

"I see the light at the end of the tunnel." Grant stopped and lowered the flashlight so Tara could stand on her tiptoes to look over his shoulder at the welcome sight.

"Did you have to say that? Even if it is literally true." She chuckled and gave him a gentle push. "Keep moving, buster."

"As you wish." He grunted when she punched him. "I'll stop with the movie lines, okay?"

"Please." She chuckled as they hurried toward the end of their confinement.

Relief and anticipation flooded through Grant as the opening neared with each stride. Relief to successfully navigate out of the inky passage. Anticipation for figuring out where on earth they had wandered to. He'd pull out his park map and compass. Then calculate their position. Soon he'd have them on the right trail again. As soon as they reached the sunlight.

Tara released his hand as they drew ever closer to the end of the tunnel and greater visibility. The last twenty feet they practically ran by silent agreement. When they emerged into daylight, Grant stopped at the edge of a steep precipice overlooking a wide valley with high hills flanking it on all sides. At the bottom, a creek wiggled its way between the trees. Several large black birds circled above the valley. At the far end, a low layer of fog obscured the ground.

"Let's figure out where we are." He removed the backpack and withdrew his tools. The handheld compass proved useless, however, when the needle slowly rotated in a circle, never stopping its arc.

Tara grabbed the bottle of water and drank a few sips, then handed it to him. "So?"

"My compass is broken." He drank and then offered the bottle to Tara, who took it and replaced it in the pouch. Grant scanned the sky and then shook his head. "I can't tell where the sun is in the sky. The light seems to come from all around. Must be the height of the hills surrounding us."

"We can't stay here so what should we do?" Tara shifted the pack on her back, running her hands under the straps to ease the weight on her shoulders. "If we find a place to eat, my load will get lighter."

"Okay, and while we do that we can sort out our next steps." Grant perused the area in front of the cave and then pointed to the left. "There's a trail leading into the valley. If we follow the river, we should eventually find civilization. Or at least a park ranger."

They hiked down the slope to the trail, and then picked their way slowly down to the bottom of the winding path between rocks and underbrush. Pebbles loosened by their clumsy steps skittered downhill.

Tara tapped his shoulder as they turned the last time before reaching the bottom of the trail. "That fog is getting worse."

Grant glanced to where she pointed and halted in his tracks. He could no longer see the far end of the valley. Scanning the area, he shook his head in disbelief. "The cave is gone."

"What?" Tara spun around to peer up the way they'd come. "That fog is rather unusual…"

Grant nodded as the layer grew into a wall of white mist, swirling and boiling into a barrier moving toward them. Almost like watching a storm front build on the horizon and advance across the sky. Except within the confines of the hollow. Odd indeed.

"It does seem late in the day for such a phenomenon to occur." Grant had never known fog to rise to obscure higher elevations so quickly. Or at all. "We should keep going before we can't see our way."

"Do you know where we are?" Her puzzled expression revealed her distrust of his plan.

"No."

"Then do you know how to get where you wanted to go?" She wrapped her arms around her waist, tapping her index finger on her elbow.

"I know that if we don't move, we'll be in the fog and unable to find anything." He held out his hand, palm up. "Are you with me?"

She stared at him, studied the approaching fog, and then slapped her hand into his and sighed. "Lead on."

"I won't let anything happen to you, Tara. Believe me." At her reluctant nod, he squeezed her hand and led her on down the valley. Hopefully not into trouble. Especially since he had no earthly idea as to where they were or in which direction they headed. Good thing he'd brought the pistol.

Chapter Twelve

"Stop. I can't go on without eating something." Tara placed one hand over her rumbling tummy. The sound echoed in the hush of the woods. "Please?"

She didn't require a great deal of food to survive, but if she didn't eat she'd end up fainting on the hard ground. Knowing sandwiches and chips awaited them, she simply could not prolong their picnic another minute.

Grant turned to look at her, skimming her from head to toe with his frowning gaze. On a sigh, he shrugged. "Fine."

She lifted one brow, miffed by his attitude. Did he not realize how long they'd been walking without any sustenance? Her grumbling stemmed from tired feet and sore legs from all the ups and downs they'd traversed. Probably even more so by the fact she hadn't eaten much for breakfast, and they'd been walking for hours. "I can't help it that I'm hungry."

"I know." He shook his head and then pivoted to survey the trail and its surroundings. "Just where did you have in mind?"

Trees and brush stretched as far as Tara could see in any direction. A few trunks from fallen trees hid among vines and bushes. Moss decorated several boulders that poked from the ground here and there among the undergrowth. The rustle of leaves hinted at the presence of small critters, perhaps mice or birds searching for food. So no sitting on the ground. She quaked at the thought. What she didn't detect, as her stomach growled again, was a decent picnic spot. But she'd make one if she had to.

She scanned the underbrush again, taking her time to consider each feature and space. "Over here. Come on."

She led Grant to one of the fallen trees and dropped onto its rough seat. The grooves of the bark bit into her buttocks but she ignored the discomfort, at least for a short while. Wiggling out of the backpack, she set it on the leaf-strewn ground between her sneakers. Opened the topmost flap and rummaged inside.

"Here?" Grant tested the steadiness of the log before slowly adding his weight. "It could be rotten and collapse out from under us."

Tara retrieved a wrapped sandwich and handed it to Grant along with a shrug. "I didn't see any signs of debris that would suggest it wasn't sound. No little piles of sawdust from termites enjoying the wood. Or even holes in the bark. Besides, some of the leaves are still pale green, so it didn't fall very long ago."

"Good point." He unwrapped the sandwich halfway, holding it in one hand as he took a bite. "You've keen observation skills."

Tara pulled out another wrapped sandwich and took several bites before speaking. The blend of the beef and cheddar with horseradish sauce filled her senses with delight as it satisfied her hunger with each morsel. Swallowing, she tossed a glance at Grant. "That's so much better. I feel more human and not such a monster."

Grant balled up the wrapper and pitched it into the open pack. "You could never be such a thing, even when hungry."

"I don't know that my sisters would agree with you." She put her wrapper into the pack and retrieved two bottles of water, handing one to him. She thought of how they'd ended up in this unknown part of the forest, not even certain they were still in the state forest. How the earth moved beneath their feet, tumbling them into the large sinkhole and then the tunnel that brought them to the valley they explored. She chuckled as she reviewed her own imagery. "Here I always thought it was just a song."

Grant lifted both brows and cocked his head to one side, staring at her as if she'd lost her mind. "What are you talking about?"

Tara laughed outright, a sound of relief and happiness. They had survived quite a fall and managed to find a way to the pretty valley where they enjoyed a quiet meal together. She'd had worse dates in town. "You know, the one where the earth moves under the singer's feet and all that?"

After a moment, he barked a laugh but merely flashed a grin before sobering. "It's so not funny. You could have been hurt or worse."

"We're relatively unscathed, so no worries." She could almost see his protective instincts twinkling in his aura. If she could read auras. Really, she didn't need to because his intentions came across clear as a pane of glass. "Ready to continue?"

He swigged from his bottle and recapped it. "Sure—" He stared over her shoulder, his eyes moving to indicate she should look behind her. His gaze stayed steady as his eyes narrowed. "Slowly."

When she did as he suggested, alarm filled her as he reached for the gun. Then a snarling growl reached her ears. She pivoted in place. Spotted the pack of five wolves standing on the path, heads low and even with their shoulders as they watched the two people. Their prey.

Four of them wore gray and black coats of fur with

massive paws and long twitching tails. The leader, however, bore a majestic air in his black-and-rust-tipped coat, three of his paws also rust, the color of dried blood, but the front right white as the moon. Five sets of yellow eyes trapped them in place. No way could she outrun the beasts. Or climb a tree before they'd rip her to the ground with those paws and teeth. The space between the wolves and them charged with tension. Tara swallowed the lump in her throat, forcing down the fear with the effort. The leader seemed to study her in silence while the others intermittently snarled and growled.

"What should we do?" She gripped the straps of the backpack, prepared to move when told in which direction.

"I'm working on it." Grant shifted beside her to load the gun.

She shot a glance at him, shaking her head. He firmed his lips and slid the cartridges into the chamber. The lead wolf raised his gaze to meet hers. When he blinked and opened his mouth to reveal sharp canine teeth and a large dark pink tongue, she sensed a change come over the pack. Was he smiling at her? She blinked twice. Detected a difference in the air as well. Almost as if the leader had come to a decision. He raised his massive head, amber eyes staring at her for several moments. She nodded to him and smiled, understanding filling her head without knowing exactly how.

Grant aimed the gun at the pack and Tara quickly laid a hand on his arm. "No. They won't hurt us."

He kept his gaze on the beasts, ready to shoot if provoked. "I'll protect you. Get behind me."

"Against five wolves?" She gripped his arm, shaking her head. She had to convince him she knew they were safe without revealing how she'd obtained the knowledge. He'd dismiss her claim as utter nonsense. Still, she had to try. Before he took a chance on pulling the trigger on an unknown and unreliable gun. Squeezing his arm, she peered into his eyes. "Trust me; they won't harm us."

He studied her, eyes dark with concern and deadly intent. "How could you possibly know that? They're wild animals, hunters. We're their damn lunch."

She chuckled which made his eyes darken even more, and his brows draw down. "Don't be silly." She glanced toward the path and the wolves and then smiled. "See, they're leaving."

Grant jerked his gaze toward the hunters that had simply turned and trotted on up the trail, slipping into the woods at the turn in the path. The lead wolf paused long enough to look back at them before loping out of sight. Grant remained on guard, searching the area for several moments. When he turned to meet Tara's gaze, she smiled at him.

"Like I said." Tara bent to lift the backpack and slip it into place on her shoulders. Glad to have the standoff peacefully resolved without having to explain. "Shall we go?"

"What just happened?" Grant checked the gun before slipping it into his belt. "I thought those wolves intended to attack when I first saw them. Why did they turn and leave like that?"

"Maybe the leader decided we weren't worth the trouble?" She giggled with relief and at the astounded expression on Grant's face. If only she had her camera, what a great picture to share on social media. Maybe not. Better to be living in the moment after all since she wouldn't want to try to explain any of their day to her friends. Or her sisters. "I don't know that for sure, since I don't speak wolf." She chuckled as she led the way down the trail, preferring not to have to endure his questioning glances which were sure to happen.

Better to keep him wondering than to reveal her hidden talents. Her keen ability to sense what others are feeling, even in animals. She could tell when a dog felt afraid and thus would more likely attack. The wolves harbored only curiosity and recognition. Strange. At least they hadn't attacked so Tara and Grant could search for the right path home. Grant needn't be bothered by the whys and wherefores. The less he knew, the better for her. And him. She hoped.

Chapter Thirteen

The unusually warm fall made sweat bead on his brow as he forged a path through the underbrush toward the narrow end of the valley. Grant rubbed a hand across his forehead and then dried it on the jeans covering his thigh. After the trials they'd faced, surely they would find the main trail and a way out of the forest. Safely. That was the key.

Without a working compass or being able to see the sun's position, he walked blindly through the trees. They followed a narrow strip of a path made by animals moving through the undergrowth. He couldn't go back the way they had come for two reasons. First, the fog continued to push them in one direction away from where it blocked out all light. Second, he couldn't tell where they had come from any longer. They were lost and he carried no functional tools to determine the right direction to seek help. The selection of tools and instruments only served as dead weight in his backpack.

"Grant, can we stop for a minute?" Tara sounded tired, her voice weaker than when they'd started on the day hike.

He glanced over his shoulder. Tara had dropped onto

the edge of a large rock half buried beneath a fallen oak tree. He strode over to rest on a log beside the boulder, examining her face for evidence of fatigue. They'd been walking for hours with few stops. Retrieving a water bottle, he offered it to her.

"Take sips since we don't know how long we'll be los…out here."

"I am thirsty." She peered at him with worried eyes and took a quick sip. Wiping her mouth with her sleeve, she frowned and gave him the bottle. "You were going to say lost, weren't you?"

He wished he could deny the charge with all his heart. Despite his training and his equipment the simple fact remained. "Yes."

She looked away, her gaze slowly scanning the surrounding barren deciduous and evergreen trees and underbrush. "Why didn't you say something?"

He perused the forest instead of looking at her. Noted the stark outlines of the branches hibernating until spring. The leaves clustered around tree trunks and bushes. Let his gaze drift anywhere but toward her for several moments. Delayed seeing the disappointment in her pretty eyes replacing the trust they once held. "I promised to protect you and I will."

Silence met his statement. Curiosity forced him to turn. He met the unblinking serious regard of the woman he had vowed to keep safe. She slowly shook her head, though not with disappointment. Instead, a hint of vexation glinted in her hazel eyes.

"You're upset." Not that he blamed her. After all, his track record appeared to be repeating itself. Failure loomed.

After what happened to Jeremy so long ago, he had studied every survival training handbook he could find as well as took first-aid classes. Scouts taught him self-reliance. He became a volunteer fireman to learn how to perform rescues. Instead of summer camp, he convinced his parents to send him to wilderness survival school. Learning how to live with the provisions of Mother Nature and his own intelligence gave him confidence. He might be rusty on the details, but he could and would get them out of their predicament even without functioning tools. But the woman gazing at him with sad eyes did not know the extent of either his capabilities or determination.

"Only that you didn't share the reality of our situation." She braced her hands on her thighs and then pushed to her feet. "I don't like being misled."

"Literally?" He stood, adjusting the pack into place.

"Or physically, but knowledge is power. Tell me that we need to look for clues as to which way to go instead of letting me follow you in circles. Two heads are more effective than one."

She had a point. But his pride still smarted. "Fine. Now you know."

Grabbing the straps of her backpack in each hand, she smiled up at him for several moments. She took two steps toward him and then took hold of his shoulder straps, pulling him to her. "Kiss me."

"After all I've put you through I don't deserve your kiss." Desire and pride battled in his chest. Her lips tempted even more when the smile softened and emphasized her full mouth.

"I do." She pulled him closer to claim her reward.

He savored the sweet touch of her lips on his for the brief moment they shared. When she pulled away he longed to drag her close again. Feel her in his embrace, inhale the scent of her sweet self. Even as he considered the possibility of following his desires, Tara had already increased the distance between them. She glanced over her shoulder as she pivoted and took two strides on the ghost of a trail, beckoning him with her smile to follow. Putting his feet into motion, he soon caught up. But had he caught her? That was the bigger question.

She held out a hand, and he wrapped his fingers around the warm flesh. If she wanted a say in their dilemma, he was all ears. "Which way do you think we should go?"

Tara took a minute to scan the surrounding hardwood forest before squeezing his hand and shrugging. "If we pick a direction, we'll eventually find someone who can help us. After all, there are always park rangers patrolling the trails."

"And people on ATVs and horseback who explore these hills." She'd been right. Together they could find their way out of the mess they were in. She released his hand and started down the path. "Let's go."

The trail wound along the upper edge of the valley. As they picked their way over fallen limbs and around tree roots, he kept a watchful eye on the mostly deciduous forest. While most of the wildlife he'd seen so far had been prey not predators, black bears, cougars, coyotes, and of course wolves, all populated the area. Not to mention timber rattlesnakes and other venomous reptiles. The threat most definitely existed in the form of the animals living in the shadows of the plateau. Best he kept both eyes wide open.

As they made their way around a bend in the trail, Tara tapped his upper arm with a playful swat. "I'm enjoying being with you, Grant. The fresh air made me forget for a while the daunting challenge Roxie laid on me. And put the event in perspective since we've gotten lost together."

"What challenge?" He grasped her forearm and tugged her a couple of steps closer. He wanted her near to him in a way he'd never felt before. And also within reach should she need his help traversing the uneven ground.

"You'll laugh." She chuckled and broke her arm free of his grasp.

"No, I won't." He took her hand again and squeezed her fingers. "Try me."

"Okay, but no laughing." She pierced him with her gaze, a light smile flitting on her lips. She slid her hand free and readjusted her backpack. "Promise?"

"Cross my heart."

"Making dessert for Thanksgiving." She sidled down the left split in the winding track along a rocky outcrop, diffused sunlight softly illuminating the uneven surface.

"How is that a challenge?" Whipping up a batch of brownies and adding a dollop of ice cream couldn't be that difficult. Could it? He peeked at her as he avoided the large rock pushing out of the earth in the center of the trail, noted her frown and nod.

"Ever since my mother died, everything I try to bake flops." She glanced at him and then to the dirt trail, one hand tapping the rocks as she went. "Spectacularly."

She started singing a campfire scout song as she walked, not entirely in tune but she seemed to be having fun. He had to admit he'd never would have guessed that taco shells could catch on fire in the oven. He opened his mouth to offer to help her with the dessert when he heard the distinctive sound of a rattler. A quick perusal of the rocky ledge she nonchalantly touched to steady herself yielded the beast's location. The beige snake with dark chevrons down its back blended with the surrounding collage of rock and stone. More disturbing was the large triangular head with staring eyes fixated on his woman. He grabbed Tara's arm to pull her to him, away from the dangerous snake coiled on the ledge. She stopped singing and playfully jerked away from him and stumbled on a root in the midst of her reflexive action. Yelped when the fangs struck her left forearm before he could complete his attempted rescue. The whole episode took a split second, not enough time for him to make a second try. Again he'd failed in his primary objective.

She recoiled into him, cringing away from the pit viper

slithering out of sight. Blood tinged the holes in her jacket sleeve. She laid a hand on her arm and stared at him with shock in her eyes. He might not be able to get rid of the shock, but he could do something about that bite.

"Take off your coat and roll up your sleeve." He dropped his backpack on the ground and searched inside for the first-aid kit. Searched his memory for the steps for treating a snake bite. The first of which was to call 911, which they couldn't. Damn. Second, to wash the area with soap and water. Like that could happen. Still… "I need to clean the wound."

After several seconds, she reluctantly pulled the jacket off and dropped it to the ground. Rolling up the torn left sleeve of the sweater, she angled her arm up to permit a closer examination of the damage.

"It's okay." She quickly gripped her arm, covering the wounded limb with her palm. "It's just a scrape. All I need is a…something to cover it."

"Keep your arm down, below the level of your heart." Damnation, he needed to think. Not stare at the pain and shock reflected in the widened eyes staring at him. Was there a hint of fear in those gorgeous hazel orbs fixed upon him? Retrieving a gauze pad, he ripped open the paper wrapper and then poured some water on the pad. "Let me help. I know what I'm doing."

"No, really, I'm fine." She eased a step away, pressing her hand to her forearm as she blinked slowly.

Why was she resisting? Did she not want him to see her arm? She seemed uneasy, nervous, as well as reluctant to comply with his directions. But what made her feel so insecure in his presence all of a sudden? Peering at her arm, he didn't see any swelling. Not yet, anyway.

"Are you wearing any jewelry?" He hadn't noticed any rings she'd need to remove if her hands became swollen, not that he'd looked too closely. Well, he had glanced at her left hand, but it wasn't like he'd gotten up close and personal about it. He'd been very relieved to see no ring on her left hand.

"Just a necklace." She angled toward him so he could see the pendant hanging on a chain around her neck.

"That's okay. If you'd had rings or a bracelet on, then you'd want to remove them." He attempted a smile, but he was too worried to drag one onto his face. "You must trust me. I'm concerned the venom will spread through your body, and you'll die."

"It just scraped me. A mere scratch." Cautious and defensive, she regarded him with a solemn tilt to her head. "Do you have a Band-Aid?"

He blinked at her in surprise and consternation while the hand holding the dripping gauze tightened into a fist almost of its own accord, forcing the water to trickle between his fingers. She wanted to bandage a snake bite and continue on their way? "What's wrong?"

"Nothing." She shook her head and stared at him, then slowly lowered her gaze to the wound site where her hand remained hiding the puncture holes left by her attacker. "It doesn't hurt."

"It may be numb from the shock." Probably not, but how else could he make sense of the situation? "At least let me take a look and make sure you're right."

"I'll take care of it. Don't worry." She peeled her hand away, revealing the precisely spaced holes made by razor sharp fangs. Holding out her hand, she raised both brows and smiled. "My bandage?"

What the hell was she thinking? Still, he didn't see any immediate signs of infection spreading up her arm. Or swelling, for that matter. The glimpse she'd afforded him left him perplexed. When a snake tangled with his old dog years before one of the first signs of the bite was the swelling. The poor beast had not survived the snake bite, even though the vet had done her best. Injecting the antivenin within an hour of the attack. The complications from the venom led to the ultimate death of his pup. Since Tara didn't appear to have any inflammation, the first sign of trouble after the bite, perhaps she spoke the truth.

"If you're sure…" At her nod, he fumbled in the kit to locate the thin paper package containing a sterile strip. He'd seen the snake strike with his own eyes, and yet the aftermath ended up nothing like he'd ever witnessed. How was that possible?

"Thank you. Now, how about you fetch some water while I apply this thing." She shooed him toward a lower ledge of rocks a little ways up the trail. "I'll be there in a minute."

Mystified. That's what he was. Could the day get any stranger? "Okay, but I still—"

"Go on. I'm fine." She pulled at the paper tabs to peel out the bandage and turned her back to him. "I've got this under control."

Dismissed, he sauntered away, hesitant to leave her alone. Vaguely aware of her keeping some secret from him. What if she collapsed despite her assurances? She'd been snake bit and brushed it off like it was a mosquito bite. Even those could prove deadly what with the lethal viruses the insects could carry. He repeatedly glanced her way, reassuring himself she remained on her feet. After a couple of minutes, she strode toward where he waited with a protein bar and water. She donned her jacket again and acted like nothing adverse had occurred.

"All is well, Grant." She unwrapped her bar and took a bite, chewing with a smile barely lifting the corners of her mouth. "Let me finish this and then we'll press on. While I was taking care of my scrape, I spotted a chimney farther down in the valley."

Grant frowned, confusion replacing the mystification. Or compounding it. "There's a house in a state park?"

"Maybe it's the park lodge or something." She took another bite and studied him. "Or rental cabins. They have those, too."

"A logical explanation." The kind he preferred over any other, especially the inexplicable and unprovable kind. "Help may be closer than we thought."

He'd give just about anything to will an escape from their present circumstances. Whoever might be in the building Tara had spotted would likely have some means of solving the problem. At this point, he wanted nothing more than to end the hike and return Tara to safety. That might mean calling for a ranger to drive them back to the car. Or lead them to the trail head. Point them in the right direction at a minimum.

Folding up the paper wrapper, Tara tucked it into her jacket pocket and then zipped the pocket closed. "Let me have some water to wash that down, and I'll be ready to go."

He handed her the bottle and scanned their surroundings as she swallowed. "It's beautiful here, but I'm longing for home right about now."

She capped the bottle and gave it back to him. "I feel ready to continue now that I have some food in me."

"After you." He motioned for her to take point and he brought up the rear as they started walking again.

The trail wiggled and wound down the side of the valley into the bottomland near a murmuring stream. Then wended its way into a clearing where a small stone house with a matching chimney issued forth a thin but steady stream of smoke into the blue sky above.

If it wasn't enough to find a residence within the ravines and hollows of what he believed to be a state park, the decorations on the exterior walls hit him in the gut.

Arrowheads sparkled among the muted tans and beiges of the surrounding stone. Quartz? He'd have to move closer to identify the type of stone used, but it glinted and reflected the light much like some variety of silica-based stone. But why would such a useful and valuable tool grace the wall of a small house in the woods? As nothing more than decoration.

"It's odd that they'd use arrowheads in such a fashion." Grant pointed toward the glinting objects, then flung his hands wide, palms up. "They are probably very old, perhaps brought by Indians hundreds of years ago to trade for beads and blankets."

"They're pretty, so I can understand having them there." Tara stopped at the edge of the clearing to scan the vicinity. "Why not use them in such a fine fashion?"

Grant halted beside her, angling his gaze to contemplate her with wide eyes. "They're too valuable to hang on a wall."

"Nonetheless, there they are. It's not up to us to judge the occupant's choices. Come on. Let's see if anyone is home." Tara stepped into the deep grass of the clearing and strode purposefully toward the house. "Hopefully, they'll have a phone."

"Or a working compass, or perhaps even be able to tell us how to get back to the car."

"Surely whoever lives or works here can help us."

Grant perused the house and its surroundings, then allowed a frown to settle on his forehead as he followed close behind her. No indication of any utility connections, no satellite dish. No vehicle or even a driveway. Nothing. What were they walking into?

Chapter Fourteen

The wispy column of smoke on such a mild day seemed to indicate somebody was cooking. Otherwise, the interior of the small house would be hot and uncomfortable. Tara scanned the house as she ambled beside Grant toward the shadowy front porch. Her heart still raced at the near miss the bite had caused. She'd begun the healing process before Grant had asked to give her first aid. Fear of his finding out about her gift replaced the shock of the bite. Thankfully, he hadn't pressed her any harder, or she would have been forced to reveal her true nature. An event she'd delay as long as possible. Maybe even never tell him. Even if she did follow her heart's desire to be with him instead of letting Beth have all the fun.

As they neared the abode, the shadows lightened, so a single chair on the porch came into view. The dark brown door stood closed between two curtained windows. The air shimmered around the house as a flock of black birds swooped into the trees edging the clearing. The wedge-shaped tails confirmed which species of black bird.

"I don't think we should go any closer." Tara stopped, laying a restraining hand on Grant's arm as she peered more closely at their avian companions flying to and fro, or perched on a limb, staring at them. The iridescent plumage, rough throat feathers, and large, sharp beaks clearly identified the birds as ravens. Dozens of them. Intently scrutinizing her and Grant as if they considered the people intruders in their territory. A shudder worked down her spine. She didn't normally believe in superstition and legend, but when it came to ravens, she made an exception.

He glanced at her and then studied the house. "Why not?"

"I've got a funny feeling all is not as it seems." She'd bet good money magic played a role in the hollow, but Grant wouldn't want to hear what she suspected. He sent off waves of doubt whenever anyone mentioned things mystical let alone magical. Indeed, he'd blatantly denied the existence of magic. So Tara would keep mum until she had confirmation. Even then, convincing Grant of her findings would prove another challenge. But if she had to, then she was prepared to set him straight on several mistaken ideas he held onto.

"Why did all those birds show up?" He waved a hand toward the uneasy flock, calling to each other as they flew back and forth. "Are they starlings or what?"

"They're ravens." She followed the birds' agitated movements for several moments. "I've never seen so many in one place before."

"They're noisy, that's for sure."

She folded her arms beneath her chest and slowly shook her head. "It's odd to have such a large flock, or rather an unkindness, of ravens. They normally pair off after they reach maturity."

Grant suddenly focused on her instead of the ravens, his brows raised as he let out a low whistle. "You know a lot about birds. How come?"

She grabbed the straps of her backpack. "I've always

loved birds, especially owls and hawks. You know, birds of prey."

"So why do you know so much about ravens? Aren't they scavengers, not hunters?"

"Yes and no. I studied them for a report I wrote for a high school English class on Poe's 'The Raven.' I wanted to know more about the bird's characteristics so I could discuss how it was represented in the poem."

Then she'd become somewhat obsessed with learning all she could about them. Much like the narrator's obsession in the poem that drove him mad. She'd learned about the myths and legends surrounding ravens, how people associated them with death and the macabre for centuries. Poe had even said that they symbolized mourning as well as never-ending remembrance, which seemed like it would be another form of obsession. The paper she'd turned in received high marks, but she came away from the exercise wanting nothing more than to not be in their presence. To have so many of them clustered in the pretty little valley unsettled her composure even more than the unknown magic shimmering in the air.

Grant tilted his head to one side and rubbed his chin with one hand. "I'm impressed. My papers weren't that specific, much to my teacher's dismay. I'm fascinated by rocks and sediment, that sort of thing. Finding correlations between igneous rock and anything literary is quite a daunting prospect, believe me."

"And to answer your other question, ravens eat a wide variety of foods. They eat carrion and small animals as well as eggs and berries. Most anything really. Even garbage."

Grant swiveled his head to watch the flock's movements. After studying them for a while, he aimed his gaze at her. "They seem to be observing us. Doing their own empirical research. It's rather unnerving."

"I know. That's freaking me out." She shaded her eyes

with a hand, watching the erratic flight of the large birds. "I've never seen anything like it."

"We can't stand here all day doing nothing." Grant drew in a breath and let it out on a long sigh. Then straightened his shoulders with a decisive movement. "I guess I should go knock on the door?"

The very idea sent chills down her spine. She inspected the stones, searching out sigils and signs within their surface. Or perhaps a pattern each stone contributed to the wall of the house. Anything to explain the magical shimmering enveloping the structure. She longed to have the nerve to confide in the man at her side. To work with him to solve the puzzle they'd fallen into. She did not want to enter the building without a better understanding of what they had stumbled upon.

But they had no other choice. Grant was right: they couldn't stand there all day. The sunlight faded with each passing moment. Would they make it to the car before dark? Or be stranded out in the woods along with the wild animals? A shiver wriggled through her. She steeled herself for what they'd discover behind the door.

She nodded and Grant strode to the porch. As he reached the bottom of the three steps, the door eased open. A bent, gray-haired woman limped through the opening, leaning on a cane. Tara peered at the woman, finally seeing what she'd searched for when she spotted the symbols carved onto the door frame and threshold. Magic did indeed exist in this clearing. In the house, more specifically. Powerful and yet subtle enough to make detection difficult. She put up a guard on her mind and heart and kept her eyes open as the frail woman moved into the diminishing patch of daylight at the edge of the porch.

She appeared to be in her eighties. Maybe older. Wrinkles and moles supported each other across her face. Ice blue eyes peered at Tara, thin gray brows arched above.

The intelligence streaming through the woman's eyes gave Tara pause. All definitely was not as it appeared. She needed to proceed with caution.

"Welcome to Raven Hollow." The crone smiled, revealing yellowed and twisted teeth. "I'm Lenore. Who might you be?"

Tara started at the name. Weird. She'd heard that name before, but where? No picture of a friend floated into her mind. It tantalized her memory. Something mystical in its own right perhaps, or dangerous. Another reason for care.

Grant returned his foot to the grass at the base of the steps as he laid a hand on his chest. "I'm Grant, and this is Tara."

Tara stepped forward when he spoke her name, a smile automatically springing to her lips. "Raven Hollow? Is that where we are?"

Lenore nodded and indicated the open door behind her with a jab of her cane. "Won't you come in?"

Gracious, the shadowy interior didn't invite. But she'd not turn tail on a little old woman and run like some frightened child. The very idea sparked determination in Tara's soul. Even if the shadows weren't stretching across the clearing, longer and longer as the sun moved closer to its bed for the night. Without a working flashlight, they'd never find their way after dark enveloped the mountains. The only real choice remained acceptance of the woman's invitation.

Grant glanced at Tara as she moved closer to him. "Actually, we need your help if you don't mind."

"We've gotten turned around and don't know how to find our way back to the trailhead we started from. Do you have a phone we could borrow?" Tara waited for the woman to finish combing fingers through her wiry gray hair. Wondered at the flick of those intense eyes up to where the ravens croaked to one another. The short bursts of harsh tremolo distinct and otherworldly, shooting another shiver of unease down Tara's spine.

"I have no…phone to lend." The crone blinked at her several times and then grinned. "But I've a lovely pot of soup on the fire to share."

Why had she hesitated? The woman may be up to mischief. Tara could detect the presence but not the origin of the spell cast upon the house and hollow. She'd keep her eyes open. "We'd rather try to find our way back. It's getting late."

"Are we still in the state forest?" Grant glanced up to the croaking ravens before addressing the woman. "How come you live here in the middle of nowhere?"

"I don't think this is a…state forest." A glint of some undefinable emotion flickered through the crone's eyes. "I've lived here for a very long time. It's my home."

"Do you live alone?" Tara saw no evidence of other people living in the hollow, but she needed the reassurance that they wouldn't be surprised. Especially by someone lurking inside the house. "You must get lonely."

"I have the animals of the forest to keep me company." Lenore exposed her crooked teeth in a flash of a smile. "They're quite friendly."

A commotion among the birds drew Tara's attention to the trees and the sky. The ravens shifted their positions constantly while the people below chatted. Almost as if they understood the disquiet in Tara's chest. Lost in unfamiliar territory with night swooping down on them with every passing second. They had to be miles from the trailhead. They'd hiked for hours. Their meager supplies wouldn't last through another day unless they gathered food from the forest. But in November there wasn't much growing, and she didn't know which plants to choose anyway. What if she picked something that ended up being poisonous? Quite a pickle.

Tara settled her gaze on Lenore, her chin angled a little to the right. "How did you come to live here? How do you survive?"

"Don't you worry, missy. I make do." The crone cackled and thumped her cane on the wooden floor of the porch. "With the help of my friends."

Tara raised one brow at the evasive answer, suppressing the urge to question her further, to unearth the woman's history and truth of her presence in such an outlandish place. Even as she recognized the urgency of finding their way out of the forest, she simply couldn't walk away and leave Lenore behind. How could she abandon the crone to fend for herself so far from civilization? She must be senile to believe she could continue to survive on her own. No, the strange old woman must have guided them to her home for a reason. Or someone had. The crone had no detectable magic of her own. The mystery of Raven Hollow deepened with each fleeting moment.

The air around the house glittered with pulsing magic, tingling her skin at the proximity to what she could only surmise was the source of the supernatural essence she sensed. She peered more closely at the symbols flanking the door. Deciphering them required more knowledge than she possessed. Something about aid, a test, and forever among other curious designs. Obviously, if she couldn't figure out what they meant, she couldn't discern a means of breaking the spell, allowing them to return home. Which raised the other reason she'd stay. To discover exactly who and what had led them to Raven Hollow and why. She'd bet her last dollar they had not chanced upon the place but had been drawn to it for some yet obscure purpose. Lenore may be old and ugly, but she hid a dark secret. Of that, Tara was certain.

Chapter Fifteen

The air cooled as the shadows lengthened on the valley floor. Grant zipped his jacket against the chill. The crone confounded him. What on earth was she doing living alone in the middle of the woods? Whether in the state forest or not, her situation remained untenable. Questions bombarded his brain as to how and why she had ended up in what to him was a worse predicament than what he and Tara faced. With night nearly upon them, he needed to decide their next move. Finding their way to his car was priority one, but how? The flashlight batteries had about given out already. He glanced at the sky, but no moon hovered above. The night would be pitch black.

Still, he should at least try. Tara's disquiet rippled over him like waves in an agitated pond. He'd find a way to see in the dark later. Maybe the woman had batteries. Then again, given her situation? Ha. Probably not. He must return Tara to the safety of her home. Somehow.

"Lenore, can you point us in the right direction to return to the main trail?" He shoved his hands into his coat pockets, fingering the practically worthless flashlight with disgust. So much for his planning skills.

"I never leave the Hollow." Lenore rested both hands on

the top of her cane. "You don't want to go now anyway. The sun has set."

Grant looked up at the darkening sky above with a swallowed gasp. The sun sure set quickly in the mountains. Good to note for the next time he planned a harebrained hike in the woods to relax.

He cast a quick glance at Tara's thoughtful expression and then regarded Lenore. "Well, if your offer still stands, we'd be much obliged if you could let us stay with you for the night."

Tara stiffened beside him, mute and rigid. She seemed determined to remain calm despite whatever bothered her. What it might be he couldn't imagine. The old woman was no threat, all hunched and hobbling. Nobody else apparently lived there with her given the lone chair on the porch. He'd stay alert to the possibility of someone hiding, just to be on the safe side. If Tara needed reassurance, then he could give her that much. He held a hand out to her, and she glanced at it before placing her own in his. She flashed him a grateful grin and then turned back to their hostess.

"Of course, of course. I so rarely have visitors it will be my pleasure." Lenore slowly spun and limped toward the open door. "We'll have some soup and bread and get to know one another."

Grant led Tara up the steps and across the aged wood floor, its patina seeming to glitter as the sunlight faded away into dusk. He closed the door behind them and helped Tara remove her pack. The holes in her jacket reminded him of her ordeal earlier in the day, and he again marveled at her good fortune to not have been seriously injured by the snake. Handing her the knapsack, he perused the interior of the cabin as he removed his own.

Two doors suggested other rooms at the back of the house. The large room he stood in included areas set aside for a grouping of comfortable looking chairs, and the kitchen with its fireplace, a table and three chairs nearby. Surprise swept through him when he spotted the fine linen cloth on the table set for three in matching china and silver. A silver bowl of nuts sat in the center of the square surface between two candles. He glanced at Tara's open-mouthed expression and then continued his perusal of the abode. She'd warned him things might not be as they seem, but he'd not expected anything like what he witnessed.

Intricate needlework pictures hung around the room. Lenore had to do something with her time, he supposed. Two or three multicolored braided rugs lay in front of the overstuffed chairs, reminding him of his grandmother's home. A large buffet stood against one wall; one drawer pulled halfway open sporting a skein of yarn hanging over the front. Copper-bottomed pots hung around the fireplace and reflected the firelight.

"You have a lovely home, Lenore." He nodded to her as she stirred what he assumed was soup in the black kettle hanging over the merry fire.

"I hope you'll find it comfortable for a time." She tapped the ladle against the kettle rim and then hung it on a black metal hook on the right side of the fireplace.

"Were you expecting guests this evening?" Tara linked her fingers around the shoulder straps of her pack, clutching them like a security blanket dangling in front of her legs. "I'm sorry if we've interrupted."

"Not at all. The ravens let me know you were on your way to visit and so I prepared a nice meal for you. I've a bedroom all fixed up for you as well." The wizened face peered up at Tara with a hint of conspiracy mixed with humor in her expression. "You don't mind sharing a bed with your handsome man, do you?"

Grant waited for Tara to explode at the concept even as concern settled in his chest. She'd planned for their visit? And expected for him to sleep in the same bed with Tara?

After all, they barely knew one another so he'd be surprised if she were willing to sleep with him. Literally or figuratively. He cleared his throat in preparation to offer to bed down on the floor, when Tara shot him a look that stopped him.

"Not at all, Lenore. I don't want to add more work to your kind offer to put up with us for the evening." Tara hefted her backpack. "Can I deposit this in whichever room is ours for the night?"

Tara surprised him at every turn. From her stance and posture, he could tell she really would rather be anywhere but in the house. Though he didn't comprehend her reasons, he admired her courage to face the situation head on. To not let her discomfort overcome her good sense. After all, they had no other option but to stay the night and then make their way home in the morning at first light.

"It's the door on the right." Lenore waved a wrinkled hand toward the room and then winked at Grant. "You'll be wanting to see where you two will sleep tonight, big fella. Now won't ya?"

Damn straight. He also wanted to have a little talk with Tara as to what she was up to. Find out what concerned her more, the actions of their hostess or the idea of sharing a bed with him. "Yes, ma'am. I'll be right back."

Tara pushed the door open and strode into their assigned quarters for the night. He halted beside her when she paused to get her bearings. A full-sized bed boasted a patchwork quilt in red, blue, and green, with a solid, dark green bed skirt. Cozy, with barely enough room for him alone. Sleeping with Tara meant they'd have to snuggle. He grinned in anticipation. Two bed pillows wearing dark green shams rested on top of the quilt. By the lone window in the room, a table held an urn and basin with a chair nearby. Did the place not have running water? How would Tara feel about roughing it? He spotted a door and hurried to it to find it led to a small bathroom. Complete with toilet and sink and even a corner shower. Though tiny, it would meet the need. He scratched his chin, contemplating how the home had inside plumbing in such a remote spot. There must be a well somewhere he hadn't noticed. Behind the house perhaps. Something to check for after dawn. He spun on his heel and strode into the bedroom where he dropped his backpack under the window.

"Not too shabby." Grant went to the bed and pushed down on the mattress, testing its firmness. "It'll do for one night anyway."

"You don't think we're going to share that bed, do you?" Tara crossed her arms and stared at him. "I mean, not both of us under that quilt."

"You want me to sleep on the floor, that's fine. I had planned to do so." He strode over to her and clasped her upper arms. "I won't do anything to make you uncomfortable."

She gazed at him and then released a long sigh. "That wouldn't be fair. You're as tired as I am, I'd wager."

After the words left her mouth, he realized how tired his body felt. "You're right, but that doesn't mean I'll force myself on you."

She blinked several times as she searched his eyes. "I trust you to be a gentleman."

He grinned, relief at not having to endure the hard floor on a chilly evening spreading through him in equal measure to the anticipation of holding her. Another surprise from his lady. "It will be like olden days when couples bundled."

She lifted one brow and shook her head. "Engaged couples did that, not friends. Or new acquaintances."

"True, but the results will be the same. We'll share a bed but not touch each other." A fib but he couldn't help himself. He slid his hands down her arms, careful to avoid her injury, and grasped her hands. "Let's go have some dinner and find out what we can about Lenore's situation. I'm intrigued by what she's doing way out here."

Tara bit her lip as she slowly shook her head. "Her story may surprise us both if she'll share it with us."

"I hope she will. I'm very curious about her. I wonder if there's some way we could help her out." Grant tugged on one of Tara's hands, dropping the other free, and led the way into the main room of the house.

During their absence, Lenore had warmed the house by adding fuel to the fire, its tongues of flame reaching up the sides of the kettle in a haunting dance of heat. "Bring me your bowl, and I'll ladle some soup into it." Lenore grabbed the ladle and swirled it in the depths of the pot.

Tara and Grant did as asked and then took a seat at the table. Lenore dished up her supper and carried it to the table, and then retrieved a loaf of warm bread resting on a silver tray and placed it by Grant's elbow. Finally, she opened a little door beside the chimney in the wall and reached inside. Grant frowned while she struggled to remove something from within the depths of what must be a pantry of sorts.

"Do you need a hand?" Grant half rose, but she waved him back in his seat.

"I do this all the time." She tossed a smile his way as she pulled out a small ceramic jar and placed it on a nearby table. Then she carefully picked up her cane before grasping the jar in her other hand. Limping to the table, she placed the jar between them and sank down on her wooden chair. Hanging her cane over the back of the chair, she blew out her breath and peered at Grant. "Whew. That's getting harder and harder as the…years go by."

"You should have let me help you." Grant picked up his spoon and scooped up some of the hot soup.

"You're my guests." Lenore glanced between him and Tara. "I'd never ask for you to work in my home."

"I was raised to offer to help no matter whose home."

Grant ate the soup, enjoying the pleasant warmth flowing down his throat. "I don't mind lending a hand in exchange for your kindness."

Lenore inclined her head a little to one side. "Your mother taught you proper manners."

Grant nodded as he scooped up another spoonful. "Emphatically."

"How about you, Tara?" Lenore pinned her gaze on the woman in question. "Did your mama teach you right?"

"She was quite a stickler for being polite and helpful." Tara's gaze turned wistful. "I wish she were here."

"Ah, I am sorry." Lenore laid a bony hand on the table, halfway between her and Tara. "The loss of a parent is often difficult to adjust to. Has it been very long?"

Tara shook her head, her ponytail swaying. "A few years. Feels like yesterday."

"Time has a funny way of distorting itself, doesn't it?" Lenore chuckled and picked up her spoon. "At least it seems so to me. After all the time I've spent in this hollow, I barely recall living anywhere else."

"How long have you been out here by yourself?" Tara stirred the hot soup, peering into the steaming bowl for a beat and then back to Lenore.

Grant looked into his vessel of delicious yet mysterious hot broth and stirred it around. What kind of meat floated among the bits of carrot and onion? Perhaps fish since the house stood near a river. Maybe chicken or some other wild fowl. Tentatively, he dipped his spoon and tasted the soup again. Interesting blend of tastes, some savory, some sweet. He couldn't quite pinpoint all of the ingredients.

"Many years now." Lenore sliced the loaf of bread with a long serrated knife, its silver blade casting off shards of candlelight when she finished drawing it through each slice. She slid the pot toward Tara. "There's honey to put on the bread, if you'd care for some."

Grant accepted a slice of bread and waited for Tara to finish with the honey pot. "Do you enjoy living here? I would think it lonely."

He honestly couldn't imagine existing so far away from the comforts and conveniences of a town, let alone his home city. No phone. TV. Electricity, for that matter. At least she seemed to have running water. Cooking over a fire instead of a stove. Probably the most glaring thing missing was access to the internet and all it enabled for both his work and recreation. He wasn't a huge fan of social media, but he did indulge in binge-watching his favorite shows and movies. He'd go stark raving mad if forced to live for more than a few days under such conditions. How did she endure?

Sadness settled in Lenore's eyes when she raised her gaze to meet his. "You have no idea how alone I feel at times. If it weren't for the ravens and songbirds keeping me company, and the wolves upon occasion, I'd have gone crazy over the years." She patted Grant's hand twice with a lopsided smirk upon her lips before picking up her spoon again and eating her soup. "Now I have people to fill the void."

A chill having nothing to do with the darkness falling outside swept through Grant. What did she mean by such a statement? Her words hinted at a desire to keep them in the hollow for her own needs, whatever they may be. Surely she wouldn't trap them in their room when they retired for the night. Would she? She ate the soup, so she likely didn't poison the pot. But what about the bowls? He tightened his grip on the silver spoon in his hand, only relenting slightly when he started bending the metal. If she insisted on their staying, would it be as companions or slaves? No point worrying about the distinction. They wouldn't be staying if he had anything to say about it.

"Tomorrow we'll need to head for home." Tara held her bread midway to her mouth while her wary gaze moved from Lenore to Grant. "Our family will be worried since we were due back this afternoon."

Leave it to Tara to make short work of Lenore's hope. Grant nodded as he chewed the deliciously sweet bread and then swallowed, examining Tara for any signs of drugging or poisoning from their meal. Where had the paranoia sweeping through him come from? He didn't normally look for the dark side of people, especially little old women. As Lenore continued to eat with gusto, his defenses lowered somewhat. His imagination obviously had run away with him. But he would maintain his vigilance.

Another tack would open possibilities without putting themselves at further risk of retaliation or duplicity. "Perhaps you'd consider coming with us? You could find a better place in town somewhere so you wouldn't be lonely."

Lenore reared back in her seat, dropping her utensil, her cold blue eyes flashing with anger and something else he couldn't define. Panic? She fisted her hands on the table top, her wiry frame trembling. She glared at him for several seconds and then pounded one hand on the tablecloth.

"Impudent man." Lenore shook her head as a frown pulled her brows down so far her eyes became shuttered. "Impossible. I cannot leave. How dare you suggest such a reckless idea?"

Taken aback, Grant could only stare at her for the span of two breaths. "What did I say?"

"If you've quite finished, it's grown very late, and I must close the house up for the night." Lenore shoved her chair away from the table and stood, leaning heavily on her cane while Tara and Grant hurriedly swallowed and stood as well.

"I didn't mean to offend…" Grant splayed his hands and shook his head. Went back over the conversation and found nothing out of line. At least not so far as he could tell. "I'm sorry if I did."

"Apology accepted. But you must be more circumspect in your opinions in my house." Lenore bobbed her gray head once, her eyes belying her age with the intensity of her regard. "They may be taken the wrong way, and then you'd not like the consequences. Now if you'll excuse me, I'll bid you both go and have a goodnight."

"Are you sure you're all right?" Tara hesitated at the edge of the table. "Do you want me to help you clean up?"

Lenore waved a skeletal hand side to side. "It's not necessary. Go on to bed. You must be tired."

"If you insist…" Grant paused, contemplating the undercurrents in the room while waiting for Tara to sidestep around the table to his side. "Thank you again for your hospitality."

He placed a hand on Tara's lower back to escort her to their shared room. Enjoyed the easy sway of her hips as they crossed the floor. When they reached the doorway, Lenore called out to him with a raspy yet steely voice. He gave Tara a gentle push to propel her through the doorway. He looked over his shoulder and saw the crone standing straight and piercing him with her stare.

"Yes?" Her posture belied her age and ailments and worried him all at one time.

"Do not come out of your room until daylight." Lenore shook a bony, crooked finger at him. "Keep your young lady safe, as you said you would."

Startled by both the veiled threat and the unexpected strength in her voice, he could only nod once. How had she known about his promise? "Understood. Goodnight."

He closed the door and turned to see Tara's worried features. While they had food and shelter, he still disliked the bad feeling in the pit of his stomach. What *had* they gotten themselves into?

Chapter Sixteen

Concern etched lines around Grant's mouth and eyes when he closed the door and looked at her. Had he felt the tension in the room? Tara suspected he detected the vibrations stirring the elemental magic enveloping the house. A spell cast over the building and its lone occupant. Lenore didn't appear to possess magic of her own but a powerful sorcerer had left behind an incantation that blanketed everything in the hollow. She must be the key to everything. But how?

"Are you all right?" Tara drew Grant's gaze with her question, a look suggesting deep confusion and disquiet. She untied the laces of her shoes and toed them off, pushing them under the bed with one sock-clad foot.

He sauntered closer, stopping when he stood near enough to touch her. But he kept his hands at his sides. His gaze drifted away to peruse the room much like a detective searching for clues to a mystery. Evaluating and inspecting each object. Touching each furnishing and piece of furniture. A frown settled on his brow when he returned his attention to her.

"You may well be right." Grant rolled his shoulders and rocked his head side to side, apparently relieving tension in his neck.

"About?" She sidled to the bed and sank onto the firm mattress. Dang, she was tired. She splayed her hands behind her and leaned on them, tempted to fall backward and close her eyes. "You'll have to be more specific."

"About things not being as they seem." He raked his fingers through his hair, leaving furrows in the luxurious mane tempting her to touch it as well. "Lenore seems odd."

Tara peered up at him from her reclined position. She'd noticed the vague replies and abrupt changes in tone and mood of their hostess. The peculiar conversation and comments. Even the house in the middle of the forest was strange. The fact that the crone happened to have the exact number of chairs and place settings for dinner also triggered a red flag in Tara's mind. Concerns she'd keep to herself for the present.

"How so?" What exactly had sparked his consternation?

He rubbed one hand over his stubbly jaw, the rasping loud in the quiet room. "She pretty much threatened me, or rather us, for one thing."

She sat all the way up to brace her hands on her jean-clad knees. "She did? What did she say?"

"Not to leave this room until daylight and to guard your safety." His eyes narrowed and he pressed his lips together for a moment in thought. "Like I promised."

Tara gripped the denim with both hands as she blinked up at him. "How did she know that you had?"

"Exactly. That's what's bothering me." Grant sighed and sat on the lone chair beside the bed. He yanked on the boot laces and slipped them off, wiggling his feet one by one. "I don't think I mentioned it."

Tara shook her head slowly, contemplating the hints and clues to their predicament. "Neither of us said a word about previous conversations or anything."

"No, and how is it she knew we were coming early

enough to prepare for our arrival?" Grant rested his hands on his thighs as he studied her with a frown.

"I know, I was startled by that, too." Tara shook her head a couple of times, recognizing the danger they had stumbled into. "We need to get out of here tomorrow."

"Soon as it's light." He rested his elbows on his legs. "You trust me, don't you?"

His serious regard reinforced the weight of the question. Something more than their current predicament seemed at play, another mystery. She searched his eyes, looking for hints as to what lay beneath his concern. Had she somehow given him cause to suspect her true nature?

"What's wrong, Grant?" She rubbed her hands on the denim covering her thighs. "There's something you're not telling me."

"It was a long time ago, but feels like yesterday." He sat up, lifting a hand to grasp the nape of his neck. He leveled unblinking eyes at her. "I won't let anything happen to you."

"I know." She hesitated to probe, but he seemed to need to get the past off his chest. "What happened a long time ago?"

He shook his head with a sigh. "Looking back, I know I couldn't have done anything, but that's in my mind. In my heart, I feel there must have been something that would have saved my friend's life."

Whoa. Commiseration mixed with a dash of guilt filled her eyes with tears. She blinked twice to force away the tears and leaned forward to reach out a hand, offering to comfort him, waiting for him to accept or refuse. "Tell me."

She watched him reach a decision, the shift of his shoulders and the angle of his chin drawing him closer to her. He placed his hand in hers, squeezed lightly and then clasped her fingers as he studied her expression. When his gaze steadied on hers, she squeezed his hand, encouraging him silently to share the burden of the memory.

"My friend, Jeremy, died while we were messing around where we shouldn't have been. I was looking at the foundation of a dilapidated old house, seeing what kinds of rocks they'd used. He went off on his own. I guess he didn't see the old well cover until he'd stepped on it. The sound of the wood giving way alerted me but too late."

"Did he fall?" If so, their situation and his reaction made perfect sense. "Like we did?"

He nodded slowly. Tears glittered in his eyes when he paused to take a shaky breath. "He screamed all the way to the bottom, about fifteen feet into the darkness."

"I'm so sorry, Grant." She wanted to touch him, hold him in a comforting embrace, but he'd put an emotional distance between them. As if holding back. She wouldn't push him to be with her, just wait for his next move. Ready to console when needed. "What did you do?"

"The only thing I could. I ran back to the trailhead to my bike, went to his parents' house for help." He rubbed his eyes, releasing a tear to slide unimpeded down his stubbly jaw, creating a path for several others to follow. "We were too late."

She stifled the gasp his confession prompted. Watching him cry in silent agony as he relived the tragedy from his youth. "Oh, Grant…"

The death of a friend at such a young age must leave lingering questions and grief. Guilt, too. She'd never experienced such a loss. Other than her parents' deaths, she had been fortunate in that regard. For a young boy to experience such a trying ordeal, striving to overcome the weight of the guilt he piled on himself for not being big enough, strong enough, fast enough to bring the necessary aid to his friend.

"It's okay. I've dealt with it." He leaned forward again to take one of her hands, examining each finger. "It taught me to be prepared for anything as best I can. Which doesn't mean I'm perfect, obviously, since I forgot spare batteries for the flashlight." He lifted his gaze from her hand to meet hers, a wry twist to his mouth.

"We're fine. Tomorrow we'll make our way out of here." She smiled to reassure him as much as herself. Would the spell permit them to escape its power? She'd find a way to ensure they did. With good fortune, without disclosing her secret. "You'll see."

He nodded and let his gaze drift around the room. "This place is like a fantasy, or a myth, or other fantastical story location. Sitting out here like some sorcerer's lair."

"At least we're warm and dry." Tara pressed her palms onto the quilt on either side of her thighs. He had no idea. She suspected some form of test awaited to successfully sever the grip the incantation held over Raven Hollow and Lenore. Grant wouldn't accept such a conclusion, not without evidence. Which she did not have. She rushed to change the subject. "Are you tired?"

"A little." A spark lit in Grant's gorgeous eyes as he sat contemplating her. "Are you?"

"A little." She echoed his words back to him, a grin blooming on her lips. Glad the mood in the room had lightened with his changed expression. "What should I use to bundle you up for bed?"

He looked at her askance with a matching smile. Several emotions flickered through his eyes as he winked. "Or should I bundle you instead?"

She laughed at his comical expression. "I don't trust you to keep your hands to yourself. So I'll do the bundling, thank you very much."

Grant chuckled and rose to his feet to cross the short distance and sit down beside her on the bed. The dip of the bed with the sudden additional weight propelled her into him. She caught herself with a hand on his thigh, warm and strong, before she hastened to pull away.

"See? You're already touching me." Grant wrapped an arm around her waist, supporting and embracing.

"No, you're touching me." She wiggled as if to move away but he pulled her in tight against his side. Her outer thigh warmed to fever pitch by his body heat penetrating the denim. His hand slid under her sweater and landed on her bare back, claiming her. She inhaled sharply and detected his tangy aftershave and a hint of man. She let out her breath in a rush, striving for calm but failing. "You're still touching me."

"Now you sound like my brother when we were children in the back seat of my parents' car." He used his free hand to smooth a stray hair away from her face, then traced the outline of her cheekbone with his forefinger.

Each stroke of his finger sent a ripple of awareness to fuel the desire building in her core. She resisted at first, reminding herself of all the reasons why she couldn't risk her heart. But the spark grew into a flame that engulfed her sensibilities and left them ashes. Turning her face to meet his hot gaze proved her undoing. His mouth only inches from hers. She moistened her lips, and his gaze landed on them for two heartbeats. Then he lowered his mouth to hers and ignited a passion neither could control. The anxieties of the day and the emotional sharing of his friend's death fed the flames, seeking relief from the stress and strain in the arms of another.

Tara devoured him like a chocolate éclair with extra dark chocolate. Kissing him everywhere she could reach while he held her wrapped in his arms as if he'd never let her go. Then he eased her down on the bed, lying with her in his embrace as they continued to explore each other. Learned the delights of playing, using the tips of their tongues like fencers sparring. They kissed for what seemed moments, but when Tara paused for air, gasping as if she'd run up a flight of stairs, she glanced at her watch. Wait.

What? She peered at the hands and shook her head. Two hours had passed. She pushed on Grant's chest, and he shifted his hold.

"What's wrong?" He frowned when she sat up and scooted a couple of inches to the side.

"We've been at each other for hours." She tapped her watch face. Was it broken? "Or at least that's what my watch says."

"No way." Grant sat up and peered at his watch. His brows shot up. "That's not possible."

She stared at him while she sorted through the facts and reflected on her suspicions. Recalled Lenore's comment about time in the hollow. "We need to be very careful while we're in this house."

He slowly nodded, eyes serious and mouth compressed into a flat line. "And we need to stay together at all times."

"I don't understand what is going on, Grant." She shifted to sit cross-legged facing him and rested her hands on her knees. "But somehow we must find our way home tomorrow. My sisters will be very worried."

They would be more than worried if they knew where Tara and Grant had disappeared. She struggled to remain calm when she considered all the ways her sisters could harm themselves in her absence. Without her there to heal them from injury or illness. Much like she ended up concerned for how to break free from the enchantment, if it were even possible. Daylight would shine on the answers in the morning with any luck. The truth remained hidden in darkness until then.

"Agreed." He laid his hands on top of hers and squeezed. "For tonight, you need your sleep. I'll keep watch."

"You need your sleep, too." She attempted to stay focused, but the touch of his flesh to hers shot desire right to her nether regions. *Breathe. Relax.* She thought about their situation and settled on a plan. They couldn't both sit up all night and expect to hike out at first light. "Wake me in a few hours, and I'll play sentry while you get some z's."

"Okay, but I have one stipulation." He leaned closer until his nose touched hers.

A smile bounded onto her lips as she searched his twinkling eyes. "What might that be?"

He kissed her, once, twice, and then smiled. "I want to hold you while you fall asleep."

Would she fall asleep with him embracing her? Touching her? Igniting all her womanly fires? Probably not, but she'd happily give it a try. "Okay."

Without another word, they crawled to the head of the bed, moved the pillows so they could slip under the quilt, and spooned together. He kissed the back of her head and loosened his grip but held fast. Tomorrow would bring new challenges, new adventures, and new risks. Of that she held no doubt. For the moment, though, Grant kept his promise to ensure her safety. Could she keep her vow to protect herself? When Grant left, would he take part of her heart with him? And if so, how large of a piece? She drew in a breath and let it out slowly, restoring calm. Riddles to be solved later. Closing her eyes, she cleared her mind like she'd learned to do when preparing to heal a particularly nasty wound. Tara's last thought before sleep claimed her was of the perfect fit of Grant's arm wrapped around her waist.

Chapter Seventeen

The following morning, Tara awoke to the soft glow of sunlight on the wood floor. Snuggled against something warm, she had no inclination to roll out of bed. She yawned and pulled the quilt tighter. Then she remembered the day's plan and pushed the blanket away. She moved to sit up but Grant's arm held her firm. They'd both drifted off to sleep instead of one keeping watch. *Damn.* She pushed on his arm to jostle him awake. He stirred and yawned, pulling her to him.

"Grant. We need to get going." She wiggled to try to break free of his embrace, and he groaned. "What's wrong?"

"Nothing that more time in bed with you wouldn't relieve." His voice sounded low and sexy and so very tempting. She longed to press against him, experience being with him the way he suggested. And yet.

"We don't have time. Let me go." Tara pushed on his arm and slowly he lifted his hand to allow her to get out of bed. "Come on, lazy bones. Time's a-wasting."

"Ugh." He blinked at her twice with his sleepy eyes before heaving a sigh. "Fine."

She chuckled as she strode into the bathroom to freshen

up for the day ahead. Ten minutes later, she and Grant were both ready to go into the main room. Opening the door, Grant waited for Tara to proceed him. She was surprised to find Lenore busily stirring something in the black kettle, her back to them while she bent over the pot.

"You're up early." Tara eased across the room, reluctant to startle their hostess. She noted three place settings of silverware and napkins on the tablecloth. "Can I help with anything?"

"I imagine you're very good at helping." Lenore glanced over her shoulder with a sad smile. "Do you ever grow tired of waiting on others?"

Tara frowned even as the truth of the statement settled on her heart. Her job at the bookstore involved assisting customers to locate books and jewelry to their liking. Her healing powers required insight into the needs of others on a fundamental level, one deep enough to escape their awareness. To her mind, she provided a service unlike anyone else. Even if it meant having to hide behind a façade of acceptability. A mask which seemed to pinch more often than not. "Occasionally, but most of the time I like to extend a hand when someone is in need."

"Be sure you tend to your own needs and desires." She tapped the ladle on the rim and aimed it at Tara, sharp, intent eyes pinned to her face. "When the time comes, you must choose wisely." Lenore raised a brow for a moment, waiting until Tara dipped her head in a brief nod, and then pointed at Grant. "Do you like porridge?"

Tara studied the bent old woman, pondering her caution but not understanding her meaning. Choose what? What time did she refer to? Could Lenore see into the future like Beth? Or was the advice prompted from her experience? Confusion weighed her brows down as she watched Grant and Lenore exchange smiles.

"Yes, ma'am." He moved closer to peer into the cauldron, sniffing. "With brown sugar and pecans?"

"If you'd like." Lenore turned to retrieve a stack of bowls and began dishing up the hot cereal. Handing a bowl to Grant, she pointed to the table. "You'll find everything you enjoy waiting for you."

Jerking her head to one side, Tara gasped at the sight of a bowl of chopped pecans, a sugar bowl, a pitcher, and a plate of butter in the center of the table. Where had they come from? Magic shimmered in the air, answering her question. Lenore needed no help when the house provided for her. Grant didn't seem to notice anything unusual. Just as well, given he'd probably try to find the reason for the magic and not merely accept the fact of its existence.

He strode to the table, placing the steaming bowl down before dragging out a chair. He added toppings to his oatmeal and stirred them in with a spoon. Concentrated on the task before him, so he didn't notice the exchange between Tara and the crone.

"Anything wrong?" Lenore regarded her with humor in her old eyes.

She knows that I know because I'm a witch. Tara accepted the offered porridge, hoping her expression didn't reveal the unease swirling in her gut. "We'll get out of your way as soon as we eat."

Lenore turned to the kettle with a shrug. "Don't hurry away on my account. I'm enjoying your company. It's rare that anyone ventures so far from the usual trails."

Tara frowned as she strode to take a place at the table. They hadn't spent much time with her. Enjoyable or not. She added butter and brown sugar to her bowl and then combined everything with a thoughtful stir of a spoon. She watched Lenore limp over to sit with them, easing onto a chair with considerable effort.

"Are you hurting?" Tara sensed something amiss in the crone but couldn't pinpoint the cause.

Lenore blinked before aiming her gaze at Tara. "Old age aches and pains are nothing new to me, my dear. I've endured them for quite a while."

"I may be able to ease the discomfort, if you'd allow me." Tara held her breath, hoping Grant wouldn't ask for an explanation of how she intended to assist their hostess. Seeing the older woman in distress tugged at Tara's conscience, prompting the spontaneous offer despite the risk of exposure. If Lenore accepted, then Tara would find a way to soothe the aching without Grant seeing.

"My pain comes from living a long life." Lenore lifted her spoon, holding it aloft as she rested her gaze on Tara. "Keep your secret safe and I'll manage."

Tara cast a quick glance at Grant. Puzzlement reflected in his eyes as he looked at her, head tilted to one side. She jerked her head once to tell him not to ask questions. Hoping all the while that he listened and kept his mouth shut. He quirked a brow at her and resumed eating, though his gaze flicked from Tara to Lenore and back again.

"As you wish." Tara spooned some oatmeal into her mouth and chewed.

"My wishes are rarely granted, so thank you." Lenore's sad smile spoke volumes.

Tara resumed eating, musing on Lenore's strange lifestyle. With so few visitors, she must relish having guests to speak with, to share a meal. How lonely would it be to live so far from neighbors? To have so few people darken her doorstep? While Tara didn't enjoy crowds, she wouldn't want to be so very alone, either.

Grant paused in shoveling his breakfast into his mouth to glance at the crone, then at Tara. "We really must go. Tara's sisters will be worried, as will my brother."

Roxie and Beth had probably searched for Tara's

essence when she didn't return as expected yesterday. Perhaps they chalked up her absence as her falling for Grant and staying overnight with him. Perhaps they panicked and called the police. Anything was possible.

"I understand." The woman's voice cracked as she stared at her bowl, steam slowly rising to obscure her sad expression. "Before you go, will you help me bring in the bags of nuts I've gathered over the past weeks? The filled burlap sacks are heavy and my back aches today."

Grant bobbed his head twice and put his spoon into his empty bowl. "Of course. Tell me where they are and where you want them."

Tara spooned another bite into her mouth to quickly finish her breakfast. She didn't care if it scalded the roof of her mouth, she wanted to finish and be on their way. She didn't want to separate from Grant for a minute while they remained in the hollow. "I'll give you a hand, Grant."

Lenore smiled at each of them, not bothering to eat. "You both are too kind. The bags are propped up at the edge of the clearing. That way I could fill them there and then drag them inside. Thank you."

Grant pushed away from the table and strode to the door. Tara hurried to catch up with him. Stopping at the top step, Grant cast an eye over the clearing until he spotted the group of sacks off to the left. "Over there."

Tara looked in the direction he pointed and then realized the hollow echoed with raucous croaking. "What's wrong with the ravens?" The whole flock seemed to be calling to each other, flapping their wings while perched in trees at the right edge of the clearing. "They're quite loud."

The thump of Lenore's cane on the wood floor announced her arrival behind them. "Don't mind them. They're just calling the wolf pack."

Tara spun to blink at Lenore, not comprehending the woman's meaning. "I'm sorry?"

Lenore chuckled, a creaky laugh that scraped Tara's nerves raw. "They're getting the wolves to help them with their breakfast." She lifted the gnarled cane to point to the ground beneath the birds. "There's probably a dead animal, maybe a deer. Their beaks are useless to open a large carcass. So they call the wolves and let them tear open the animal and eat what they want before the ravens take the rest for themselves."

Grant bristled beside Tara. Waves of concern washed over her senses, alerting her to his agitated state. He tossed her a glance and then studied the woods. His expression revealed he didn't much like the idea of wolves nearby.

"I don't see them." He bit out the words in a rough voice.

Lenore tapped her cane on the porch floor. "Give it a little while."

"In the meantime, Grant, let's get those sacks inside." The sun was high in the sky already. Time seemed to be in overdrive in Raven Hollow. Or they were moving slower than usual. Either way, they needed to hurry.

They went to the group of burlap sacks bulging with pecans, walnuts, and hazelnuts. Tara inspected the number and size of the sacks and frowned.

Grant considered the bags for several moments before looking at Tara. "I count ten sacks. Lenore has been very busy."

"They look heavy. I don't know that I can lift them even though they're not large." Tara's heart sank at her inability to shorten the task by assisting Grant. "Maybe there's a wheelbarrow?"

"Wait here for me." Grant stepped forward to heft the first sack onto his shoulder with a low grunt. "Don't worry. This won't take long."

He strode to the house and went inside. While she waited for his return, tapping the fingers of one hand on her crossed arms, the ravens caught her attention. Still croaking and flapping, creating quite a frenzy of sound. Movement in the shadows of the trees on the opposite side of the clearing made her frown in concentration, trying to see what moved, and then she gasped. The black-and-rust wolf led his pack into view, milling around the presumed carcass of the poor dead deer bound to be their meal.

The idea that the birds cooperated with other species to prepare their meal fascinated her. They worked together to provide for the entire unkindness, the whole family as it were. A thought that reminded her of the dinner she and her sisters planned to prepare for their extended family. If she and Grant could find their way home soon. Thanksgiving was tomorrow after all. They had to make haste to return to Grant's car if they had any hope of sharing the holiday with their family.

Years ago, the holidays had always been times when the family and close friends without local family gathered together around the big table in the dining room; all its insert leaves in place to extend it to its maximum length. She could practically smell and taste all the delicious dishes of savory vegetables, the roasted turkey, glazed ham, and freshly baked rolls. A time of shared love and happiness. Except for the occasional drama of some kind, a simmering tension waiting to explode the happy occasion into shards of anger and hurt. Tara frowned, recalling her mother's quiet words to the injured party. An aside which worked to calm the dissent and restore the day's pleasant atmosphere. Holidays weren't always perfect, but the time together meant more than any small squabbles. They'd come together to share a meal they each had contributed to in some way, big or small.

Sure enough, just as Lenore had said, the wolves ripped open the deer. She couldn't bear to watch after the first ripping and crunching sounds reached her ears. Grant appeared on the porch about the time she turned away from the sight. He grimaced as he reached into his pocket and pulled out the pistol. As far as she knew, it was still loaded. She hoped he wouldn't feel a need to use the antique weapon. No good could come of firing such an old gun.

"Grant!" She waved her arms in the air to attract his attention. "No!"

He sauntered toward her, the gun in his hand at the ready. When he reached her side again, he shrugged. "Just in case I need to scare them away."

"Don't shoot them. They're only here to help the ravens." Tara pleaded with her eyes. "Promise me you won't hurt them."

He regarded her for several moments, his gaze flitting across her face. "As long as they don't threaten any of us, then fine."

"Thank you." Relief flew through her being. The wolves seemed more intelligent than typical dogs, more canny and aware of the people as well as the birds.

"But if they do, then I'll fire to protect you." He put the gun into his waistband and gave her a quick kiss. Then he hefted the next sack onto his shoulder and walked toward the house.

"You promised not to hurt them," she called after him.

"Only if they don't hurt you." His wicked chuckle drifted across the span of meadow to her.

She'd have to make sure he kept his word. Pacing after him, she planned her strategy. One that got them out of Raven Hollow. Soon.

Chapter Eighteen

The ravens' cries died away, leaving the sounds of the wolves snarling and chewing to fill the hushed clearing. Grant's longer stride devoured the distance to the stone house. As he disappeared inside, Tara mulled over possible ways to break away from the valley. The problem remained in not knowing the exact nature of the spell. Perhaps if she studied the sigils on the door frame and threshold, she could glean the necessary information. Tara reached the steps as Lenore started down, her cane wobbling with each step.

"I'm grateful for your help." Lenore peered into Tara's troubled eyes and grinned. "It's a happy coincidence that you stumbled into Raven Hollow when you did."

Coincidence? Not likely. Events seemed to have conspired to bring her and Grant to the valley. And then to hinder their departure. Or had Lenore made up the aching back to prolong their stay, miss the window for escape? Had she missed a chance to choose wisely by not insisting they depart rather than carrying in the sacks?

Tara's resolve strengthened with that thought. "Glad to be of service. But we must go soon. I worry so about my sisters when I'm not there to he…help them."

Lenore patted Tara's shoulder with a bony hand, her long nails discolored and chipped. "Family is important. I hope you succeed in getting home with all speed."

While the crone's words suggested she cared, the way she said them made Tara's spine crawl with anxiety. A thread of insincerity underlay Lenore's sentiment. She seemed to want to keep them with her. Something flickered in her eyes, testing Tara's resolve to find an escape from the magic holding them in the hollow. Distorting time as well? Hard to say how long they'd been trapped. One day? One week? Longer?

"As soon as we're done with the nuts, we'll get going. Don't fret." Tara, however, did worry that her limited ability with spells would hamper their efforts to find a way home. If only Roxie were there, she would have a better grasp on the type of enchantment in effect.

"I'm fine if you stay as long as you like." Lenore rapped her cane on the bottom step, making a soft thudding sound. "I never mind visitors."

Suddenly a raven swooped past Tara on its way up to perch on the porch roof. Tara peered at the haughty and seemingly defiant bird as it cocked its head this way and that, observing her.

Lenore tapped her cane on the step again, sharp raps that seemed to echo in the ensuing silence. "Get off my roof, raven. You know better than to hang over my head in such a manner."

The raven croaked three times before extending its wings to take off and fly away to join the others in the trees.

Tara sucked in a breath as her memory yielded where she'd heard her hostess's name. Why hadn't she recalled sooner? A chill began in her legs and swiftly rose to shiver up her spine and shoulders. Poe's poem. Lenore was the name of the lost love of the narrator. The woman he was destined to see, as the raven quoted, nevermore. No coincidence led them to Raven Hollow. Something or someone needed them to come, to resolve the puzzle of the enchantment on the woman standing beside her and everything else in sight. But who and why? And most pressing, how did she break the spell?

Grant emerged from the open door of the cottage and trotted down the few steps to stand with them. His gaze traveled to the wolves, a hand resting on the butt of the gun. He looked so handsome, so strong and ready for action, Tara could only stare at him for several moments. Drink in the vision of a gorgeous hunk of a man's man. One who seemed to feel for her the same attraction pulling her to him. Only problem was that it was like the clichéd moth to a flame in which the flame ultimately burned the moth. She simply didn't know if she could survive such heat.

"You have no need to worry about the wolves, Grant." Lenore blinked up at him with a snaggletooth smile. "Trust me."

He lifted a brow as he peered down at her. "Why? They're wild animals. Look at how they're devouring that deer. They could easily do the same to us."

Lenore shook her head as she aimed her gaze at the wolves. "They were invited by the ravens. They'll eat their fill and leave."

"Better safe than sorry." Grant patted the pistol handle, resting his hand on it. "I'll keep this within reach until they're gone."

"Have it your way." Lenore sighed, staring at the brutal scene.

"Shall we get started?" Tara asked, anxiety making her voice harsher than normal. Between the bloody sight across the way and the cold realization of how trapped they may be, she needed to unravel their predicament. The sooner they made an attempt to escape, the sooner she might figure out what summoned them in the first place.

He turned to address her as Lenore started limping toward the remaining sacks.

"We'll get this job done and head out." Grant held out a hand to Tara.

Taking his hand, she walked silently beside him across the open grassy area. They caught up to Lenore as she hobbled slowly over the uneven turf and around a lone sapling growing to one side. The seed likely had been carried by the wind from the surrounding woods to drop in that exact spot. Landed in a fertile depression and then began to grow and reach for the sunlight. Once its roots had established a firm connection to its environment, its stalk started to grow and flourish until it stood about ten feet tall. As long as the sapling received the proper support and nourishment from its surroundings, it would continue to grow and mature. Much like a person finds a place to live and prosper. The mechanisms behind how nature worked amazed and delighted Tara.

The crone had established her roots in the hollow. Away from every convenience. Away from every person. Away from witnesses.

The big question remained. Why?

The old woman suddenly cried out as she stumbled and pitched forward. Grant caught one arm, and Tara hurried to grab Lenore's other to steady her until she regained her balance. Tara sensed a gap within the crone, a kind of disconnect inside separating her into two beings? Or somehow divided against herself. Lenore gasped several times, sucking in air as she propped herself on her cane with both hands.

"Are you all right?" Grant peered at her with a frown between his eyes. "That would have been a nasty fall."

"I'm fine. I twisted my ankle on something." Lenore shook her head slowly, her breathing slowing to normal.

"Can you walk on it?" Tara sensed the woman was in

pain but not seriously injured. Not in need of Tara's healing. "You should probably elevate that ankle to avoid swelling."

"Would you mind helping me inside?" Lenore lifted her gaze in spurts until she met Tara's.

Tara stifled the unease simmering in her veins. She had nothing to fear from the old woman, all bent and crippled from arthritis. The division within proved another matter. She kept a firm hand on the woman's bony arm, enabling a span of time to deepen her probing, supporting the crone's slight weight as she rocked a little side to side.

"Of course not." Grant braced an arm around the woman's shoulders. "If you need me to carry you, I can. You couldn't weigh much more than those sacks of pecans."

"If you'll each take an arm, I think I can walk." Lenore's eyes glittered as she lowered her lashes, watching where she placed her feet.

Warning bells rang, adding to the red flags flying in Tara's mind. When she grasped the old woman's arm with both hands to ensure she could support her, she sensed a flow of magic so strong she nearly let go. But Lenore would fall if she did, so she persisted despite her reluctance. With each step they took across the field, the ravens grew louder until the air echoed with their cries. Warnings? Tara glanced at Grant, noted his serene countenance, and then felt foolish for her misgivings. After all, Lenore was merely a lonely old woman living in the country. They'd finish helping her and then find the car. Simple.

Only if Tara ignored the bells and flags. Had Lenore stumbled on purpose? If so, then why?

She spun ideas through her mind, searching for ties between them that would explain her motivation and purpose. Tara hadn't experienced any discomfort or side effects from the food and drink they'd shared with her. Nothing terrible had happened to them since they arrived in

Lenore's hollow. Even the pack leader had welcomed them in his own way, leaving them to go about their business without interference. Then why this unease flowing through her veins?

They reached the porch and headed toward the open door. As Grant ushered Lenore inside, the ravens took flight, diving and swirling back and forth overhead. Agitated and ruffled, they flew over the house, their calls reverberating and compounding into a cacophony of sound.

As Tara eased the door closed, she peered up at the birds, searching for the cause of their disquiet. She spotted several that seemed to focus on her as they swooped past, iridescent plumage glistening in the fading sunlight. The sun had dipped beneath the surrounding hills already. Frowning, she observed the ravens' frantic activity for several moments. Were they trying to tell her something? Finally closing the door all the way, she pondered the situation. Came up with no solid answers. She latched the door shut and turned to lean against it, watching Grant assist Lenore to sit in a chair and prop her foot on a pillow on another.

With the sun already setting, they'd be forced to stay the night. Again. Had the old woman led them into another trap?

Chapter Nineteen

G rant straightened from making sure Lenore's foot rested comfortably on the pillow. She seemed frail and fragile, and his protective instincts surged to the fore. Tara leaned her back against the front door, silent and frowning.

"Guess I'll go finish bringing in the bags." He crossed the room to Tara, stopping in front of her. "Why don't you get our packs from the room?"

She raised both brows as she pushed away from the door. "No need."

He frowned, puzzled. "Why not? We're not leaving them here."

"We're not leaving." She shook her head slowly and sidestepped around him. "The sun has set."

"Time passes quickly around here." Lenore folded her hands in her lap, watching them. "But I have discovered that you'll find everything you want if you'll stay and be content."

Now he really was confused. He had no desire to remain in the valley any longer than necessary. They'd just had breakfast a few minutes before. Right? He consulted his watch only to find Tara had it right. Evening approached.

"What the hell? That can't be." He strode across the

room and yanked open the door. Damn if the sky had begun to darken. He stepped out onto the porch, wondering about the wolves and the birds. He scanned the clearing and noted two things. The ravens were busy at the carcass, but the wolves had prowled closer to the house. In the fading light, he saw their silhouettes more than any details of color.

He didn't like it. Didn't want the large, savage beasts so close to the house. To Tara in particular. What were they going to do? He couldn't think of anything good they'd do so near to the stone building. One thing he knew for certain. He'd make sure they didn't come any closer.

Sliding the pistol from his waistband, he prepared to fire a warning shot. He slipped a paper cartridge from the little tin of ammunition and shoved into the cylinder. Inspecting the weapon, he noted a spot of rust on it here and there, but not enough to worry about. He'd just fire once into the air, not at the wolves. He'd promised not to hurt them and so he wouldn't risk hitting one. Shooing them away from the house would let him sleep better, too.

The pack nosed about the clearing, stopping now and again to investigate a sound or scent. When the black-and-rust beast halted and lifted his head to stare at Grant, he shivered. Those eyes unnerved him. Even in the dim light, the hulk of the wolf remained impressive. Best to clear them out before dark while the ladies were safe inside. One shot ought to be enough.

He pointed the gun into the air and pulled the trigger. Nothing happened. Damn, it misfired. The wolf glared at him as Grant quickly fumbled another cartridge from the box, spun the cylinder to load it, and then raised the gun skyward. The pack fanned out, watching him.

A flash of light above his head was followed by a loud explosion. But not the kind he'd hoped for. Pain blasted through his entire body when the pistol backfired, exploding in his hand. Pain and heat combined to make him yell.

Dimly he was aware of the wolves and ravens evacuating the hollow as he sank onto the hard floor, his feet on the steps below. He cradled the injured hand in the elbow of his other arm, striving to keep from passing out while he rocked. He didn't want to look, to see how mangled his hand may be. Kept his eyes shut trying to wrangle the pain into submission, so he could breathe without wanting to cry.

Running footsteps behind him alerted him to Tara's presence beside him. "What happened?"

He opened his eyes and shook his head, unable to speak for the agony rocketing through him. Not waiting for an answer, she moved to stand in front of him on the lower step, gingerly reaching toward his hand. She hesitated, a split second glance at his face, and then placed her hands on the wound. He jerked back at the searing ache and the stinging sensation.

"Don't." Grant bit out the one word and then clenched his teeth to stay conscious. Tried to blink away the flashes of blue and white in his eyes from the shafts of pain crashing through him.

She bit her lip and shook her head. Studied him for a heartbeat and then squared her shoulders. "You have to let me help you."

"First-aid kit." He indicated with his head to check his backpack. He hoped she'd understand because speaking was near impossible while in so much distress.

"I can help you, if you'll let me." She stared into his eyes and stood her ground. "Let me see."

Pulling his arm toward her, she forced him to show her the wound. He didn't want to look at the charred flesh, the splinters of metal embedded in his skin. Nor the blood. But with his hand right in front of him, he had little choice.

Tara examined the damage and then glared at him. "Do not move. No matter what else you do. Understood?"

"What?"

"What am I going to do?" Tara studied him, searching his eyes with a cool appraisal.

He bobbed his head once, needing to know her intent so he could brace himself for the anticipated pain. He didn't want to faint in front of her, for crying out loud.

"I'm going to heal it." A flicker of concern flashed in her eyes as she swallowed, her gaze intent on him. "Don't move. I mean it, Grant. Trust me."

"Heal it?" He swallowed to keep from crying out when he angled his hand to inspect the palm. Or what should be his palm. Instead he saw raw flesh and splinters of metal sticking from the wound. "How?"

"We don't have time for this, Grant." Tara shook her head slowly and her lips pressed into a straight line. "You must believe me when I tell you I can heal it. Don't ask me how."

"Why not?"

She inhaled and released a long breath, searching his eyes. "You won't believe me. Just hold still, okay?"

Her touch had always soothed him, so why not? He nodded once and then watched in surprise as she took another deep breath and let it out slowly. Then laid both hands on the injured hand. Again the burning and stinging started while his vision blurred and distorted. He gritted his teeth and forced himself to hold still. To not pull away as instructed. He didn't know what good she could do, but he'd given his word.

Minutes dragged by in which his skin turned alternately hot and cold, prickly and then peaceful. She closed her eyes as she moved her palms over his hand, hiding from view the site of the wound. He tried to peek around her hands but then decided he didn't want to see. After several minutes elapsed he realized the pain had subsided. Then stopped.

Tara lifted her hands from his and massaged them as she inspected his hand. "Better?"

He stared at his hand. Blinked. Looked up into her

guarded and tired expression and then back to his normal, healed hand. He turned it over to check the back, then the palm. Had he been dreaming of the explosion and now awake? His pulse raced as he tried to make sense of the last minutes.

"What did you do?"

She sank onto the porch floor beside him. Ran a hand over her forehead and then through her tousled hair. "I healed it just like I said I would."

"Am I dreaming?" Or had he experienced another miracle? He mentally chided himself for the flash of whimsy. There must be a logical explanation. He studied Tara's wary expression with a growing sense of deep unease.

She fidgeted, brushing hair from her eyes and giving him a sidelong glance. "No."

"I don't understand." His hand had been burned and bloody. He examined it again, finding nothing. Not even a scar to bear witness to the explosion that still rung in his ears.

"You don't need to." She sighed and stood. "Let's go inside. It's getting late."

She offered a hand to help him up but he brushed her aside. He didn't know what exactly she did, but he needed time to reflect and make sense of it. He needed some time and distance to put his thoughts in order. There must be a logical explanation; he just needed to find it. Gaining his feet, he led the way inside, avoiding contact. Seeing is believing, and yet. His hand bore no marks of the accident. How had they disappeared?

Lenore greeted them with a worried frown. "What was that horrible noise?"

Tara shot him a glance and then sighed. "Grant scaring himself."

He aimed a disbelieving stare in her direction. "The wolves, not me."

Tara cleared her throat. "Whatever. Lenore, I'm afraid we're going to have to beg your hospitality for another night. The day has gotten away from us."

A slow smile eased onto the woman's cracked lips. "I'll make us some supper."

Her expression stirred wary apprehension through his body. Between the vanishing wound that Tara overlooked mentioning to their hostess and the greedy appearance of that very same hostess, he needed to stay vigilant. Alert. And most of all, on guard.

Chapter Twenty

"We will miss Thanksgiving dinner tomorrow, dammit. Roxie will be mad. Probably thinking I skipped town to avoid her directive." Tara stood at the edge of the bed, hesitating to slip under the covers alongside Grant. Especially with him glowering in her direction. "Stop looking at me like that."

"Like what?" He sat up, his pillow behind his back, watching her every move. Still wearing his clothes as they'd done the first night in case of any sudden emergency.

She puffed a sigh. How could she describe his expression? The distrust fringing his eyes that followed her. A stern set to his jaw. Vertical lines between his dark brows. Shoulders high and tight even as he appeared nonchalantly relaxing in bed. He'd been taciturn ever since they'd retreated to their room for the night. Short answers to questions and silence in between. Rigid and defensive. He'd break if she lifted a finger without warning him first.

"Never mind." Spooning with him was out of the question in his current state of mind. For that matter, laying in the same bed didn't entice either. Talk about a cold shoulder. He was more like a popsicle. "Maybe I should sleep on the floor?"

Surprise replaced the wariness, but he simply gazed at her in silence. Blinking slowly as he studied her. The slow rise and fall of his broad chest screamed a willful self-control hiding the agitation inside him.

The closeness they'd shared seemed to have vanished. Sure, she'd pushed him away at first, afraid to let him in. Had hoped he'd save her from herself by dating her sister. But over the past few days, she'd seen him strong, loving, caring… She'd experienced how wonderful his arms felt around her, the smell and taste of him. She wanted it all back. But how?

He suspected she hid secrets from him. His expression shouted his doubts about her, who and what she was. He'd emphasized that he didn't believe in the supernatural, the inexplicable, in things without seeing them to believe in them. Even when he did see them, he didn't have faith in them. That was the crux of the problem. Somehow she had to make him see, make him understand, and make him agree that what he'd watched happen had in fact occurred.

He'd asked her repeatedly to trust him, and she had. He needed to trust her. For him to have faith in her, she was going to have to be totally honest with him. Her stomach lurched at the thought. Her palms dampened and she clenched them into fists of determination. She had to tell him. Had to persuade him to see her not only as a woman but in the form of her secret nature, as a witch. Knowing his reaction would then inform her next steps.

"Grant…" Crossing her arms, she considered her words carefully. He raised one brow and cocked his head, waiting for her to continue. "Listen, there's something you need to know about me."

"Yes, Tara?"

She dragged in a breath and blew it out, bracing for his reaction. But she must know if he could acknowledge her talents as fact. If he could accept her. He needed to know the truth. Then they could sort out whether they had a future. Tucking her right hand beneath her left elbow, she crossed her fingers for luck. If he didn't take it well, she'd lose any chance of a relationship, let alone a future, with him.

"About your hand…" Could she do what she needed to? Would he run from the room, and from her? She chewed on her lip for a moment before shrugging resignedly. "It's true."

"What is?" He scrunched his brow into a puzzled frown. "I don't know what you're talking about."

"I have special gifts." What a lame statement. Argh! Pressing her eyelids closed for the span of a breath, she tried to calm her thundering pulse. She opened her eyes to meet his steady regard. May as well plunge in with both feet. "I mean, I can heal people."

"I know you're a midwife. I think that's a respectable profession and calling." He rested his hands in his lap, fingers loosely linked on top of the quilt. Feigning ease and relaxation. "You delivered Pat last month without a hitch."

She waved off his observation. She couldn't force the right words of explanation to come out in proper order for him to understand. Perhaps she should start over. "No, more than that."

He tilted his head to squint at her, listening intently to what she was saying but apparently not understanding. "More than what?"

She huffed out her annoyance with herself and her lack of communication skills at the present moment. Another tactic might work better to help him fathom the reality. "Do you remember when we danced at Halloween?"

He nodded, shifted his hips on the bed to a more comfortable angle. "We had fun that night."

"Do you also remember how I danced real close and ran my fingers up and down your temples?" She could see him processing the question, searching his memory of the party and the dancing. She recalled the zing of electric current passing through her fingers into his brain and up her arms. The tumors had evaporated with only a few minutes of contact, then the current became an attraction and she'd forced herself to sever the link.

"Yeah, I thought that was a very sexy thing to do." He grinned at her, reliving the pleasure they'd shared at the costume party. He waggled his eyebrows at her. "A real turn on."

For her as well, but she knew even then the result of their foolish allure to one another. It simply couldn't work unless they could find a middle ground for beliefs neither had any intention of changing. They stood at an emotional and logical impasse. He wouldn't leave the city with all its conveniences and she wouldn't leave the small town where she'd grown up and her loving sisters resided. He wouldn't concede the existence of anything supernatural, and she knew it existed because she was part of that realm. That didn't mean she wouldn't fight for the opportunity to test those precarious waters. To see whether they had any chance of negotiating a relationship based on honesty and trust.

"That was actually the second treatment for the tumors in your brain. The first happened at the Golden Owl when I touched you. The tumors had tangled in your optic nerves so much they were difficult to remove. But your headaches eased some. Do you remember that?" She peered at him, noted when he stilled and stared at her. "The night of the dance, I finished eliminating the tumors. After that moment, the headaches stopped, right?"

"While we danced. Right." He moved his head up and down in slow motion, keeping his gaze fixed on her. She fidgeted under the weight of his regard. She steeled herself for his reaction. A reaction which would reveal whether they could make a relationship work. "I hadn't pinpointed the moment. Until now. You say you healed me? How?"

"I touched you, just like I did earlier this evening with your hand. Like Beth's migraine the other night. That's my secret gift, one I don't share with everyone." Her heart quailed when his brows rose to his hairline. "I'm more than a healer. I'm a witch, Grant."

He blinked rapidly as he stared at her for several silent moments. "A witch? There's no such thing as magic, or spells, and such."

"No, you're wrong. It's true." He didn't believe her, as she feared. A chill worked through her as if ice water flowed in her veins when he pushed himself more upright against the pillow to stare at her. Could she make him believe? "I have been able to heal by touching the wounded or diseased all my life. Since I was a little girl."

He shook his head. "It can't be. You're pulling my leg, right?" Flinging the covers off, he got out of bed. "Why are you pretending to be something you're not?"

There it was. His flat denial of her reality. The dart to the soul when her true being and abilities were dismissed as nothing more than dust. Her heart sank. She'd hoped so much that he'd see her side of the equation. Would be willing to walk in her shoes and comprehend who and what she was. His stubbornness galled her into action. She couldn't give up. Not yet.

"Oh, Grant, please believe me." She needed him to listen, understand, and most of all truly come to terms with her ability. "I care about you but you have to admit the truth. To me, but most of all to yourself."

"What truth is that?" He practically snarled the words at her.

The man she'd grown to care for, indeed the beginning flutters of love had flitted through her heart, stood glowering at her. Hands on his hips and brows pulled low to shadow his eyes. Dimmed the light of his soul as he waited for her to answer his demand. He'd transformed into a skeptic and cynic right before her eyes. She'd always told him the truth, and despite his overbearing nature she would continue to do so even if he didn't want to hear it.

"That I am a witch as well as a woman." She dropped her arms to her side and waited for his response. Fingers still crossed on her right hand.

"I don't believe in the mystic and magical." He blinked slowly at her, regarding her for several tense moments. "I thought you knew that."

She nodded as she took a step toward him. Stopped when he took a step back. "Grant, think about it. The night of the party, you saw my grandfather's ghost."

"Ghost? I thought that was some prank Zak pulled for fun." His eyes knit together as he seemed to fight with himself on whether to stay and talk with her or turn and walk away.

"No, Grandfather Patrick was there. My sisters and I helped Paulette and Meredith send him back where he belongs." Tara uncrossed her fingers, a silly and useless superstition to try to make her hope prove valid by crossing them in the first place. "You were there. You saw him. But you don't believe what you saw."

"How can you think that when someone dies they still live without a body?" He shook his head and pursed his lips, his entire body tense and ready to flee. "It's not possible, nor logical."

"Magic, just like ghosts, is part of our world. Just because we can't explain how they exist, doesn't mean they don't." Tara widened her eyes, willing him to believe. "I'm proof that magic exists."

"That does it." He strode to the end of the bed, stopped and glared at her. "I can't be with someone who would believe in such crap as magic and witches."

His words zinged straight to her heart, shooting down her defenses. Her hopes. Surely he didn't mean to be so cruel. Didn't believe what he'd flung at her. Yet he'd said those hurtful and hate-filled words. Her pulse raced and her palms dampened. She rubbed her hands on her denim-covered thighs. He had to believe her. She wouldn't let him go without a fight, not after all they'd been through and had come to mean to each other. Before she'd healed him. Now she didn't know whether they meant anything to one another after all.

"Seeing is believing?" Tara folded her arms over her chest, aware of how quick and shallow her breathing had become the more Grant grew agitated and defensive. "Is that what you're saying?"

"Exactly. I don't believe in supernatural elements and all that bull." He propped his hands on his hips; legs braced to turn and walk out. "It's just aspects of the world we haven't fully explained yet, not magic or the mystical."

"Then you have every reason to believe me because you saw me heal your hand." His words cut her to the quick. He had no right to denigrate her in such harsh terms. Tara curled her fingers into fists of growing anger. "Right before your eyes."

He shook his head as he raked his fingers down through his hair to grip the nape of his neck. "I saw nothing of the kind. There's an explanation for why my vision blurred, and things changed, just like there's a reason why the days are passing so quickly here. I merely haven't found the answer."

"Yes, you have. You don't want to accept the answer you've found." Her anger flared in her chest, warming her from the inside until she feared she'd burst into flame.

"Magic?" He laughed without humor in the sound. More disbelief. "How can you believe in such a fairy tale?"

Calling her essentially a work of fiction hurt more than she ever thought possible. Not believing in something was a fundamental and personal right. But to denounce her beliefs simply because he didn't agree? Not only was such a stance rude but disrespectful. The disrespect in his statement made her hackles rise in defensive anger.

"I'm not a fairy tale, Grant." She glared at him and then splayed her hands in front of her, inviting him to assess her entire being as both woman and witch. "I am, however, a talented and effective healer who uses magic in her work. I am a witch."

"Tara…" He rubbed the stubble on his chin for several seconds, shaking his head slowly. "If you want to believe that, then I can't stop you."

He refused to accept who and what Tara claimed to be. But his acceptance of her was the thing she craved the most. Despair replaced the anger. Her heart shredded into searing fragments. She sensed the powerful magic at work in the hollow and the house in particular. She fought the sudden urge to run, escape Grant's disbelief and disparaging looks. It was too late and too dark to attempt such a foolhardy thing. But come morning, she'd find a way to get them out of the enchantment. Away from the crone and whatever held them prisoners. Then go home and try with all her might to put her heart back together again.

She snatched a pillow and comforter off the foot of the bed and dropped them on the floor before Grant could stop her. "Tomorrow we're getting out of here."

"We said that today and failed to make good on our conviction." Grant sidled to his side of the bed and sat on the edge, looking over his shoulder at her. "I agree we need to leave without fail. We can't stay here in the woods forever like Lenore."

About Lenore. The woman seemed content to live in the little house without a steady companion. Relying on the kindness of strangers who happened by. Or had the spell reached out, searching for someone capable of breaking the enchantment? But without knowing the reason behind the spell, Tara had no way of releasing the old woman from its grip. If in fact she read the signs and sigils correctly and interpreted their warning and lesson. The set of signs indicated harsh punishment for anyone interfering in the lesson to be learned. The sigils suggested the test had something to do with humility. She wished yet again for Roxie, with her talent for casting spells, to be there to help her understand. Like everything else in her life, she'd have to muddle through as best she could on her own.

"She's not as she seems, either." Tara shook out the blanket and laid it flat on the wood floor, then tossed the pillow to one end. She caught Grant's perplexed gaze. "I can't put my finger on why I feel that way, though."

"More unexplained situations." He pulled the cover over his legs as he lay down in the bed. "I want to get back to civilization as soon as possible. This whole adventure is more than I bargained for."

"Adventure is one word for it." Debacle might be a better one. She sank onto her makeshift bed, wishing they could sleep together as before. But as long as he denied the truth in front of him, what he had witnessed, they had no future together. He had no respect for her and what she did. Better to end whatever their relationship had been and go back to her quiet life. Alone.

Chapter Twenty-One

*L*ight slowly replaced the darkness. Grant peered at the window, relieved as dawn arrived and he could stop pretending to sleep. Listening to Tara's even breathing as she lay curled up on the floor under the window. Her slight frown in sleep marred her pretty features. Desire speared through him, making him shift restlessly. So many questions flew through his brain, rapid fire and stinging.

Questions regarding their dilemma, the mysteries of the hollow, the history of Lenore's dwelling in the valley. But most of all why Tara would make up such a far-fetched lie about healing him because she was a witch. Up until that moment, he'd been planning on asking her to be his woman. They shared so many interests and enjoyed a lot of the same things. Perhaps they might have had a future together given time. Not now. Sadness washed over him at the thought. When he could see clearly across the room, he flung the covers off and rolled out of bed.

He'd slept in his clothes in case sudden flight proved necessary. Anything could happen, and he would not be caught flat-footed and unprepared. Lacing up his boots, he glanced up at the sound of Tara stirring. She sat up, yawning and stretching her arms above her head for a moment. Then she looked at him, the warm greeting in her eyes morphing into a wary expression. She pressed her lips together with a shake of her head, and then she scrabbled to her feet.

Scrambling the blanket up into a messy bunch, she shoved it onto the bed and then tossed the pillow beside it. "Ready to rock and roll?"

God, but she was beautiful even with her jeans and sweater all rumpled and her long, curly, brown hair tousled about her shoulders. Her hazel eyes still held remnants of sleep as she raised her brows, waiting for his reply. He thought he was falling for her, falling in love with her, until she threw cold water in his face by way of announcing herself to be a witch. Like that was possible. Why the charade? She probably didn't want a relationship with him. She'd even suggested he date her sister, so he'd found his answer. *Move on, bub. The lady's not that into you.* A decidedly depressing thought.

"Grab your stuff and let's go." He strode over to the chair to grab up his pack. "We're done hanging out in Raven Hollow."

"Right behind you." Tara crossed the floor to lift her backpack from its resting place. She turned to aim determined eyes at him. "I so want to get out of here."

After the events of the previous day, he couldn't agree more. He nodded and moved to open the door. Holding it, he motioned for her to precede him through it. As she stepped past him, he inhaled her sweet scent, and a pang of regret stabbed him in the gut. Still, she'd made her choice, and he'd made his. They'd have to learn to live with their decisions. He followed her into the main room and detected coffee and cinnamon, two of his favorite aromas.

"I trust you both slept well?" Lenore busied herself pouring mugs of coffee for each of them. She hobbled toward him, a toothy smile on her wrinkled face.

She reminded him of his grandmother before she died from cancer. Thin, emaciated even, yet feisty until the end. He'd not been able to say goodbye to his grandma, a regret lingering in his heart. Surely he could do something to make Lenore's last days a little nicer. Show his appreciation for her kindness.

"Fair." Grant accepted the mug she handed him and took a long sip, letting the hot, fragrant liquid slide down his throat. The pain helped him wake up more fully and be alert to his surroundings. He had to succeed in his mission to protect Tara even though she had become delusional. "I'm afraid we're going to have to leave now."

Tara sipped her coffee, her gaze flicking between him and Lenore. When she focused on the crone, a slight frown dipped between her assessing eyes. What did she think as she studied the woman? Not his problem. His task remained clear. Get them out of the hollow and on their way, or die trying.

"Lenore, we appreciate your putting up with us for so long, but now we really must be on our way." He sipped again, and then set the cup on the table. Which he noted was set for three with toasted cinnamon raisin bread, a yellow cheese wheel on a board, and a bowl of fresh cherries. A gleaming knife lay beside the board. A weapon or merely to slice the cheese?

"After breakfast, surely." Lenore wiped her hands on her apron before employing her cane to limp toward him. "You can't possibly expect to go hiking out of here on an empty stomach. I won't hear of it. Sit, sit."

He started shaking his head before she'd finished speaking. No way would he delay their departure. That path led to them constantly being hindered until they ended up stuck for another night. "Really, we have to leave now." He looked at Tara, raising his brows to ask for her agreement. "Right, Tara?"

Tara nodded and then took a gulp of coffee before placing her mug beside Grant's. "We've overstayed our visit. My sisters will be beside themselves with worry. I must get back to town to let them know I'm okay."

"But I made your favorites." Lenore attempted a smile, but it wilted from her lips before fully forming. "Please don't go."

"We must." Grant perused the bent woman, noted a slight tremble in her shoulders. Suppressing some emotion or another? It didn't matter. An urgency built in his chest, pressuring him to walk out the door and never return. "Now."

Lenore's lips pressed together into a flat line and tears stood in the corners of her eyes. She gripped the head of her cane with both hands, leaning heavily upon it for support. "If you must, then so be it."

Grant swallowed his apology. Time to lead Tara home. Then be on his way. Away from all of the craziness he'd endured over the last three days.

"Come on, Tara." He hefted his pack to slip it on, then hesitated with it in both hands as Lenore limped over to the hearth, back turned and head bent. Was the crone crying? *Ah, hell.* He couldn't leave her in such distress. Man, how he detested tears. He cut a glance at Tara who shrugged and slipped one strap of her pack onto a shoulder. Then an idea popped into his mind. A way to leave on better terms for his peace of mind. "Wait, give me your pack."

Tara tilted her head as her hands froze in midair. "Why?"

"What's left of our picnic? Anything?" He pulled the pack off her shoulder and rummaged inside.

"Enough for our lunch on the hike out." She frowned at him, arms crossed over her stomach. "Why?"

"We still have the bars." He pulled out the two sandwiches, checked to ensure the sealed packages remained intact, and a slightly crushed bag of cheese crackers. He peered at the meat and cheese, noting no change in their appearance. "Okay if we leave these with Lenore as a thank-you gift?"

She blinked at him for several moments, obviously mulling over his idea, and then grinned. "Fine with me if the sandwiches are still good."

"I believe so." Her smile coupled with the twinkling in her eyes made him want to kiss her.

He leaned toward her but caught himself, spinning away before she could guess his misguided intention. He'd shut the door on a relationship with her, so the physical connection also must end. *Damn.* He hated the idea of never touching her, never kissing those tantalizing lips. Enough. The decision had been made. Straightening his shoulders, he eased over to where Lenore dabbed at her eyes with the corner of her apron.

"Lenore, we'd like to thank you for your hospitality by giving you a little something." He held out the stack of sandwiches with the bag of crackers on top. Waited as she slowly pivoted to stare at him, tears on her cheeks. "It's not much, but it's all we have. We'd like you to enjoy these."

Lenore blinked slowly as her expression shifted, becoming lighter and happier with each passing second. Lenore stared at him as he placed the offering in her hands. She clutched the gift to her so hard he thought she would crush everything.

"Careful." He extended a hand, prepared to help if she needed him to take the items away. "You may mangle the sandwiches that way."

"Oh, my gracious. Thank you! Thank you! You have no idea how much this means to me." Lenore smiled at him through her tear-filled eyes, exposing her misaligned teeth in a wide grin.

Not the reaction he expected. "You're welcome."

"Grant…" Tara sauntered toward him, cautiously.

"Is something wrong?" Grant turned to address Tara only to see her eyes widen and brows shoot up. He pivoted his head to see what had surprised her and raised his brows. "Lenore, are you okay?"

The woman trembled violently, the sandwiches and crackers crushed to her chest. She needed assistance, so Grant stepped closer to support her, gripping her bony upper arm. Something akin to a mild electric shock pulsed through his fingers and up his arm, but he couldn't release his grasp. Not only did the current act like a shock, locking his fingers in place so he could not let go. But he also didn't want to. If he did, the crone would fall. He braced her with a hand on her back, finding her cool to the touch as her legs wobbled, barely keeping her from falling.

"Grant, no!" Tara ran over to his side and grabbed his arm, tugging to try to free his hand. "Stronger than I expected. Hold on."

Lenore's entire body shook, her hands falling open and dropping the wrapped sandwiches and crackers to the floor with a thump and crash. A whooshing sound grew in the room, and he could've sworn he heard a bell ringing in the distance building into a crescendo that overpowered his senses. Lenore's eyes lost focus, staring through Grant as though he didn't exist. She straightened from her habitual hunch and raised both arms, reaching toward the ceiling with outstretched hands. The current zipping through him grew stronger as Tara chanted unintelligible words and yanked once, twice, three times before Grant could finally free his hand. He stumbled backward several steps, taking Tara with him. He blinked at the scene before him.

His eyesight must be on the fritz again. He blinked to clear it, but the strange vision remained. The kitchen blurred and shimmered like a watercolor painting dissolving. The walls and floors and ceiling all disappeared until the three of them stood in the grassy clearing, surrounded only by the forest. The crone had transformed into a young woman, with long black hair cascading to her waist and smiling blue eyes. A crown rested on her head, displaying a mass of glittering jewels resembling the arrowheads. Her fair smooth skin and even, pearly white teeth added to the stunning effect. Beautiful barely described her. Stunning in an otherworldly way. An angel or perhaps a regal fairy queen. He blinked, hoping against hope he was dreaming. Or having a nightmare. Something to explain what exactly stood beaming at him with a wide smile.

The unkindness of ravens swooped into the clearing, flew around the trio and then soared up and into the trees. Perched on branches, they flapped and croaked, creating a raucous yet cheerful chorus. Their iridescent plumage shone in the morning sunlight, bright and full upon their backs and wings. They peered at the people, tilting their heads first one direction and then the other before yet again calling to one another. Grant surveyed the commotion, sensing the birds did more than communicate. They seemed to celebrate. But what?

"Tara, are you seeing what I'm seeing?" He shot a worried frown at her, then stared at the vision of the woman resplendent in a flowing gown of purple silk. For that had to be what it was. A dream. A vision. Surely not real.

"If you see Lenore as a young, beautiful princess, then yes." Tara folded her arms and smiled up at him, one brow lifted. "Seeing is believing, right, Grant?"

He'd always believed in the mantra. Empirical evidence had served him well for his scientific analysis of rocks and minerals, stratification and sediment. But apparently seeing didn't necessarily equate with believing. With that being the case, then perhaps one could believe in something without being able to see it. Like God, or Santa Claus. Or magic?

He glared at her and sighed. "I have no clue what has happened, Tara. Even after seeing it with my own eyes."

"Seems to be happening quite a lot lately. You must admit you can't explain everything you see, Grant." She grinned smugly at him and then turned to Lenore. "Would you care to tell my dumb-founded companion what we both know just happened?"

"I'd be delighted to." Lenore nodded her regal head with a beatific smile on her lips. "It's quite a tale. Long ago, a sorceress placed an enchantment over me to teach me a lesson…"

Grant opened his mouth to deny the existence of witches, then snapped it shut when Tara raised a brow in his direction with a quick shake of her head. Perhaps he'd said enough. Now he obviously should listen.

Chapter Twenty-Two

The expression on the man's face satisfied her almost more than his kisses. He appeared stunned and abashed as he stared at Lenore with wide eyes. Tara observed the pair, the play of emotions on each of their faces as they stood silently regarding each other. Tara had been confused but finally understood the mystery of the woman's existence in the forest. She anticipated a good story to come as to how and why the beautiful lady had been enchanted. But would Grant face the truth or deny it yet again?

"Did you learn the lesson she intended?" Tara smiled at Lenore, knowing the answer even as she asked.

"Indeed, I did." Lenore folded her hands in front of her for a moment. "Thank you so very much." Tears glistened in Lenore's eyes as she sauntered toward Tara, hands outstretched. "You have both saved me."

Tara clasped the offered fingers and felt Grant stiffen beside her. "We are glad to have been of assistance."

"You'll need to be more forthcoming than that." He cleared his throat and shifted to one side when Lenore glanced at him with laughing eyes. "What exactly did we do?"

Lenore giggled, a light, airy sound filled with joy and relief. "Only freed me from two-hundred years of imprisonment."

"Wow. That's a very long time. I'm glad we stumbled into Raven Hollow." Tara squeezed the lady's hands and then released them. "What kind of incantation were you under?"

The weight of Grant's glare made Tara chuckle. He needed to wake up and smell the magic in the air.

"A terrible curse, but one I know now I fully deserved." Lenore bowed her head as she interlocked the fingers of her hands in front of her long, stately skirt. After a pause, she lifted her gaze to encompass Tara and Grant together. "Back when I was a girl, I was a horrid person. Too selfish and haughty to consider the needs or feelings of others. I insisted on being treated as the princess that I am. Or was. I was haughty and arrogant and filled with a need to put others down to make me more important."

"I can't imagine." Knowing what she did about the crone's willingness to help and her kind hospitality, Tara had a hard time picturing this beautiful young woman as behaving poorly to others. "What do you mean?"

"No matter who did what for me, I was ungrateful and demanded even more from them." Lenore pressed her hands to her stomach. "I was never pleased or satisfied with anyone's actions or comments. Not even my father's little gifts he'd bring home to try to sweeten my temper. When I was disappointed, I threw horrible tantrums and meted out unwarranted punishments on my servants."

"Sounds like some people I know today." Grant shook his head once and leveled his gaze on Lenore. "Power can go to a person's head and make them do some strange and terrible things."

"Exactly why she cast the spell." Lenore inclined her head toward Grant, acknowledging the wisdom of his observation. "I deserved to be punished, although at that time I did not agree."

"Who cast the spell? An evil queen?" Tara chuckled at her little joke.

"My aunt, a most powerful sorceress, cursed me to live as you saw." Lenore's sad gaze drifted from Grant to scan the clearing and finally light upon Tara. "She loved me enough to want me to be a better person, a more caring princess, a more compassionate leader of our people. Alas, it took so very long for the lesson to be learned and the right people to come along to release me from my prison. As I said before, not many visitors have happened by. The animals, the ravens in particular, have kept me company for all these years. They knew you were the ones most likely to free me. For that, I am truly grateful to them."

"So what broke the spell?" Grant sheepishly glanced between Tara and Lenore. "I know, I'm admitting they exist. But what exactly did we do to save you?"

"I passed the test my aunt devised so very long ago." Lenore's expression sobered. "The touchstone, or test, of whether I could learn to be grateful and compassionate toward others. I had to wait for a generous person to think of my welfare without me demanding it. Or asking or hinting. Without me doing anything to prompt or trick them into doing so. Believe me; I tried to trick the last person who happened by."

"What did we do exactly?" Tara had surmised the spell Lenore was under had a way to be broken, but had not been able to riddle the answer. Not until Grant suggested an offering of sorts.

"You gave me your food. A thank-you gift, you said, indicating you cared about how I had treated you. An act that brought such happiness and relief I can't describe the feeling." A tear trickled down Lenore's left cheek. "Then you, Grant, touched me to help me when my body trembled with such heartfelt gratitude I could barely contain my emotions." She turned her gaze to Tara and smiled. "Then you touched Grant and your healing powers flowed through him and into me, and that magnificent, selfless act freed me. I say again, thank you."

The woman had been trapped in a crone's body for centuries, in the middle of the woods, waiting. Needing someone to offer a gift, a helping hand, without her asking for either. Surely she didn't see very many visitors in all those years, so the opportunities would have been, at best, rare. Imagine the uncertainty and despair she must have felt in equal parts for a very long period.

Lenore sidestepped to stand before Grant, reaching out her hands. He hesitated, obviously unsure whether to permit contact, but slowly extended his hands to let her clasp them with her long, slender fingers. He startled enough to bring a smile to Tara's mouth.

"Grant, I understand you do not trust what Tara has told you about magic and witchcraft." Lenore's striking blue eyes searched Grant's pale gray ones for two heartbeats. "But you must open your mind and your heart to see your future clearly. Indeed, you must accept her for the person she is for you both to find true happiness together."

He peered at Lenore for a few seconds in silence. Released from her grasp, he took a step back and toward Tara. "I believe in the empirical method of science. Keen observation leads to findings. So I suppose, as you say, I should trust what I've seen for myself. But how can I trust what Tara has been telling me?"

"You must have faith in the woman you care for." Lenore studied him as she nodded. She glanced at Tara and splayed her arms wide. "If you cannot, then you can never reach your destiny with each other."

Grant turned to regard Tara with wide eyes and a slightly open mouth. He blinked several times, snapping his lips together to press them into a line. "Tara, I want to believe you are telling me the truth, but you must realize how hard this is for me to accept."

"Have I ever lied to you?" Tara folded her arms and moved away from his rigid frame. "Ever?"

"No. You haven't." Grant looked at Tara for several moments, a slight lift to the corners of his mouth. He swiped a hand through his hair and slowly shook his head. "Then I owe you an apology, Tara. I should have believed you when you confided your secret to me. I should have trusted you to tell me the truth."

Tears sprung to Tara's eyes and she blinked, releasing one to cruise down her cheek. She swiped it away and swallowed the rest. "Yes, you should have."

Grant moved closer and took her hand in his big, warm one. "I'll never doubt you again. I promise to see you as both a woman and a healer who uses magic."

"That's all I ever asked, Grant. Thank you for believing in me." Tara squeezed his fingers with a slight smile on her lips. Then she caught Lenore's eye with a wave of her free hand. "What will you do now? Do you want to come with us?"

Lenore shook her head and then looked up at the hushed ravens sitting in the trees. With a slow lift of both arms, she raised her hands toward them. The birds rose as one into the sky, circling slowly overhead. Lenore clapped three times and then waved as the ravens paired off and flew away in different directions. Within moments, they had gone, leaving the valley quiet and serene.

Lenore lowered her gaze to Tara's. "I shall die in peace."

"What?" Tara blinked rapidly, trying to comprehend the other woman's acceptance of her death. "But you have your whole life ahead, don't you?"

"I've lived too long already. It's my time despite my

outer appearance." Resignation filled Lenore's eyes. "But you and Grant do have your lives ahead to look forward to. If you follow the river upstream about three miles, you'll find your car, Grant."

"Only three? I thought we'd gone much farther." Tara glanced at him, spied his own surprise in the revelation.

"The Hollow existed in a different dimension in space and time, making it all the more difficult for you two to have found me."

A different dimension. That explained a lot. The time flying by. The unkindness of ravens cohabitating in the small clearing. Ravens?

"Lenore, did the ravens lead us here?" Tara nodded, anticipating the other woman's answer.

"Yes, they were my scouts, my little helpers, which is how I knew you were approaching." Lenore smiled at Tara. "They listened to your conversation and shared it with me."

"That's how you knew of my promise to keep Tara safe." Grant glanced up at the sky, searching for the birds but finding only songbirds flitting about in the pretty valley.

"So they distracted me while Grant discovered the overlook spot, right where the ravens wanted us to be." Tara grinned at the cleverness of the ravens. "The portal into the other dimension and eventually Raven Hollow."

"Very good. The portal had to be opened at the right time to allow you entry." Lenore smoothed her hands on her gown as she glanced at Grant when he gasped. "What?"

"The earthquakes…" Grant rummaged in a pocket of his knapsack, finally pulling out his compass. He held it before him, peering at the face as the needle circled and then stopped. "It's working again. How——?"

"The ravens sensed my saviors were converging and the spell caused the earthquakes as the means of opening the portal to permit you both inside. So you might say magic brought you here, led you here, and now that the spell is broken it has released you back into your dimension." Lenore folded her hands together and regarded Tara, a gleam in her eyes. "Go on. You've a life to live."

"If you're sure…" Tara hated leaving the woman alone again in the middle of the woods without even a house. She glanced at Grant and then to Lenore. "Where will you live?"

The air shimmered around Lenore, softening her image as she smiled and nodded. "Do not worry about me, Tara. My time has come. Go in peace and love, my friends."

A veil lifted behind Lenore like a theater curtain pulling aside to reveal a gathering of beings, sparkly and shifting side to side, a seductive dance, as hands reached toward Lenore. Beckoning her to join them. Tara sensed they waited for Lenore, to welcome her home among her family and friends. Slowly, one heartbeat at a time, Lenore's substance evaporated into the cool, autumn air. Her essence lingered for a few beats of Tara's heart, then dissipated until she could no longer sense the woman's presence. The curtain fell into place, concealing the other realm from view. A beautiful way to pass into the next life. Tara closed her eyes for a moment, wishing Lenore a tranquil existence after her trials. The cry of a hawk sounded overhead, and she opened her eyes to watch it slowly soar across the bright blue sky. Then she dropped her gaze to meet Grant's.

"I guess we should be on our way." Tara scanned the clearing, silent and empty. "There's nothing to keep us here anymore."

Grant heaved a sigh. "One thing before we go."

"Can't we get out of here and then talk?" She'd become anxious and restless, as if something were pushing her from the site of the vanished little stone house and its mystical occupant. They no longer belonged.

"This can't wait." Grant pulled her to him, holding both her hands as he contemplated her for a moment. "I want you to know I'm sorry I didn't believe you. I want to learn more about your abilities. But most of all, I want to kiss you."

She lifted a brow. "Thanks. Okay. I want to kiss you too now that you've admitted you were wrong."

"Don't rub it in." He tugged on her hands, closing the distance between them until her chest pressed against his.

"Only for a day or two." She winked at him then sucked in a breath as his head dipped toward her.

His lips conquered hers in a demanding, ravenous kiss. She returned his ardor, wrapping her arms around his neck to capture him in her embrace. A woman starved for his taste, the feel of his hands on her back, holding her close. The world melted out of her awareness for several glorious minutes of passion shared between a man and a woman. Only slowly did reality encroach and have them gasping for air, grinning like fools at each other in the grassy meadow.

Grant slid a hand down her back and then clasped her hand. He led her over to where they'd dropped the backpacks, helped her put hers on, and then wiggled into his. All while exchanging secret smiles.

"Ready to go?" Grant held out a hand, waiting.

"Am I ever." Tara placed her hand in Grant's, and they started walking toward the river. "I can't wait to hear what my sisters have to say about our disappearing act."

Chapter Twenty-Three

The trail wound upstream between steep walls of rock and scrub brush. Tara huffed behind Grant's determined stride along the rock strewn path. The top of the incline came into sight, and she sighed with relief. It seemed like they'd been hiking for hours, but her watch said it had only been at most one. Outside of the spell-bound hollow, she could believe what she saw on its face. But she had to keep up with Grant's quick march. He'd increased the distance between them inch by inch as her energy flagged. *One foot in front of the other. Just keep walking.* Her mantra as she trudged up to the top and then stopped.

"Grant." She barely had breath to say his name. Dragging in air, she tried again. "Grant."

He looked over his shoulder and then halted, turning to face her. "Are you okay?"

She shook her head and beckoned him closer. Her pulse thundered in her ears as she leaned forward and braced her hands on her thighs. Her heart beat against her ribcage, gradually slowing with each passing minute. "That was some climb."

"We've got to keep going, or the sun will set and we'll be wandering around in the dark." He scanned their surroundings, the sun halfway to its bed, crossing the azure sky without a hint of clouds. "Lenore didn't think it was far."

"I hope not. I'm sick and tired of playing nature girl." She grabbed the ponytail holder and pulled it out. Ran fingers through the damp tresses, shaking them out to lay on her shoulders. Long shadows of the tree trunks lay across the path. Indicating late afternoon? Not again. She had no desire to relive the time weirdness of the hollow. "Are we even going in the right direction? Does anything look familiar?"

His gaze landed on her hair and then slid up to meet hers. "You should leave it down more often."

She cocked her head to one side and sighed. Not what she cared about at that precise moment. *Men.* "Thanks. Answer my question."

Grant fingered several strands, keeping his attention on her. "Fine. Despite the fact I think you have beautiful hair, I'll answer your question."

She lifted one brow and waited. Not patiently, tapping her fingers on her elbow.

"We're going the way she told us to go, and since we had fallen so far into that sinkhole, it makes sense that we have to climb to reach my car."

She glared at him, annoyance simmering in her core. "You do realize magic had a part in our fall? It may have only felt like we fell a long way?"

"I think we're on the right track, so let's keep going." He winked at her, dropping her hair to her shoulder. "Trust me."

The hint of interest in his eyes softened her resistance enough that she nodded. When he looked at her like she was a fine dessert, she couldn't help but fall a little bit more in love with him. And he was right to continue. Surely they'd reach the trail head before too much longer.

"Lead on. I don't want to spend another night in the forest."

She followed him down the other side of the hill, winding gradually down to a level stretch of trail. Around them, birds flitted about. Unseen creatures rustled the dried leaves along the trail. The smell of cedar and pine and the distinct aroma of fresh air created a heady concoction. One she'd gladly replace with the scent of her home.

As they hiked around a bend in the path, Grant suddenly gave a yell of happiness. He glanced at her, pointing ahead. "There. The trailhead at last."

She peeked around his broad shoulders and saw the brown park sign in the shape of an arrow. "Don't stop now."

She pushed past him and walked as fast as her legs would carry her toward what she considered her salvation. They'd spent days in that blasted hollow. They'd freed Lenore from the spell and done their proverbial good deed. Time to return to Roseville and normalcy. Taking the short path from the main trail to the parking lot, she burst into the clearing with its gravel area. Grant's car waited for them. She'd never been so happy to see a vehicle in all her life.

"Thank goodness." Grant strode up beside her and cut her a look. "I am sorry we missed the family dinner, though."

"Me, too, but at least we can go home now." She grimaced, aware of the lengthy explanations facing her when she walked into her house. Would they believe that she hadn't made up such an outlandish tale as they had to tell? Would Roxie believe she'd come to grips with being herself no matter what others had to say? The moment Grant had acknowledged her gift had opened her eyes to the realization she needed to be true unto herself before anyone else could accept her abilities. She exhaled, relief and frustration mingling in her sigh. "Hopefully in time for some leftovers at least. Come on."

Grant kept pace with her, fishing in his backpack side pouch for the car keys. He pressed the fob to unlock the doors, and they both got inside without delay. Tara picked up her phone and turned it on, pleading for a signal. After a few moments, she stared at the date and time on the screen. How?

"Grant, what day does your phone say?" She turned to peer at him, disbelief reverberating through her soul.

"I dunno. I didn't bother taking the time to look at it since we're in such a hurry to get back to town." He pulled his phone from his pocket and unlocked the screen. Blinked twice and then snared her with his gaze. "Tuesday?"

"That's what mine says." She regarded him for several astonished moments. The three days they thought had passed had in fact only been one. "Time was most definitely doing weird things in Raven Hollow."

"Yeah…" Grant started the engine and shook his head. "Just be glad we're out of there."

"I am. Drive." Tara didn't know whether to be relieved that they hadn't missed Thanksgiving or not. "I need to get home."

He glanced at her as he slipped the vehicle into gear and pulled out of the parking lot. "You still have to make dessert, don't you?"

"Yes." She stared unseeing at the blur of trees passing by her window. She had less than an hour before Grant would drop her off at her house. Time in which to make a decision as to what on earth she'd do about dessert. She had to make it the next day to give Roxie and Beth the kitchen on the big day. No way would she dare step foot into the kitchen with them. She glanced at Grant, determined not to let her entire family down. "Now to figure out what I'm baking."

As the car slowed to turn onto the main road, a pair of ravens perched on the stop sign, side by side, their eyes fastened on her as if they recognized her. Their adventure had begun with just such a pair of omens following her. Fitting for them to usher them on their way. Still, she'd prefer if they'd leave her alone. She blinked, and they suddenly took flight, their wedge tails and ebony feathers disappearing into the distance.

"I'm sure you'll make something wonderful." He cast her a sideways glance and then focused on the road.

Tara sat in silence, mulling the possibilities. Recalling the way the ravens cooperated with the wolves to identify and essentially prepare a meal. Remembering Lenore's tale of never being satisfied with what others did for her until she'd been punished for centuries. How she'd learned to be thankful for the efforts of others. To first be true to herself. The lessons about reaching out for help when needed or desired. Not to show weakness or inability, but to evoke a sense of community, of friendship, of family. The very concept of being grateful for the people around her and not judgmental of them.

Before long they reached the outlying country neighborhoods surrounding Roseville. Twilight had descended during the drive. Several houses boasted strands of Christmas lights twinkling on roofs and in the trees and bushes. The holiday season had arrived, and this year for the first time she would not be alone. She had Grant, who cared for and about her.

She swiveled her head to contemplate him. The epitome of a good man. Caring, strong, supportive, and yet willing to fight for what he believed in and to protect those he loved. A mix of hidden talents and obvious strengths. She could never find another man who enticed and enthralled her on so many levels. He'd proven capable of keeping his word, taking her seriously, and being there to support and guide her. From the first day he'd returned to Roseville, he'd been kind and considerate. And sexy as hell. Tempting her at every turn. Helping her when she needed it, whether she asked or not. She recalled his reaction to the kitchen when he'd first entered her home. Maybe she should find out what other talents he possessed.

"When you were in my kitchen, I got the impression you know something about cooking." Tara aimed her querying gaze at Grant. "Like baking?"

He nodded, shooting her a quick half grin. "One of my specialties as it so happens."

"Don't toy with me, Grant." Hope blossomed inside at his revelation. "I'm in serious need of help and fast running out of time."

"My mother made sure I knew how to take care of myself before I ever left home. You know, how to do my laundry, clean my room, and feed myself." He steered the car around a curve and then glanced at her. "Including baking everything from cookies to cakes to pies."

Images of working in the kitchen with her mother floated through Tara's mind. She'd assisted more than led, but together she and her mom had whipped up some amazing recipes. Her role fell to pulling together the ingredients for Peggy to use when she needed them. Tara had watched, fascinated and proud, as her mom stirred, fried, blended, kneaded—whatever the recipe demanded. They had been like a well-oiled machine. She knew the moment her mother would need the next bowl or spoon, so she barely had to pause in performing her kitchen magic. Suddenly, Tara understood why her efforts had fallen short.

"I helped my mother, but I never made anything on my own." Tara peered at Grant, willing him to understand. "I didn't learn to make anything. I learned to be the assistant."

He smiled at her, a brief twist of his head to regard her before turning forward. "I can help you this time so that you're doing the main part and I'll assist you. Together we can rule the dessert world."

"Would you?" She didn't have to do it alone. Beth had already told her that, but she'd ignored her sister's advice. What had Beth seen when she'd touched Grant that one time in the kitchen? She'd said for Grant to follow her lead. As in to offer to assist Tara? A chill flashed through her as she realized her sister's vision proved true. She stared out the windshield for a heartbeat, as Grant turned onto her street. "I'd love to cook with you."

"We can shop tomorrow morning for what we'll need, and then spend the rest of the day baking up a storm." He halted the car in front of the Golden house, the engine idling. "How about if I pick you up at ten?"

"I have to work in the morning." She leaned over to pull her backpack onto her lap then took hold of the door handle. "How about one?"

"Noon at the bookstore and I'll take you out to lunch before we go shopping?"

"Perfect." She leaned over to give him a kiss before opening her door. "I'll see you tomorrow. And Grant…"

"Hmm?"

"Maybe we should keep the whole Raven Hollow escapade our little secret?"

He laughed, a burst of deep merriment and relief. "Fine by me."

"I kinda thought so." She kissed him again. "Who'd believe it anyway?"

"Right. Love you." Grant gripped the steering wheel as his eyes widened and he swallowed hard. He blinked helplessly at her for several moments.

"Was that an oops?" She leaned down, one hand holding the passenger door open with a death grip. "Or are you serious?"

He regarded her for a moment, lips pressed together,

and then a slow, sexy smile grew on his tempting lips. "After all we've been through, how could I not love you? You're incredible and beautiful. Yes, I mean it. I love you."

His words zoomed into her heart and held firm, starting a slow fire simmering in her core. The season of joy and hope began with three simple words that meant so very much when spoken with sincerity.

"Then you should know…" She hesitated, not from fear of her next words, but to relish the feeling consuming her. Swimming in her veins and fizzing up her belly like a draft of fine champagne. "I love you, too. I'll see you tomorrow."

"Best date ever." He grinned at her, and then flicked a wave at her. "But no repeats, okay?"

"Absolutely. Bye." She closed the car door and watched her new boyfriend drive away. Then she remembered. He planned to go home after Thanksgiving. Hundreds of miles away. The very reason she'd attempted to resist his allure. She'd failed on one hand, but succeeded on the other. Her heart fell the more she thought about the obstacles a long-distance relationship faced. Not just miles, in fact, but also the length of time between seeing each other, talking in person, and between kisses. How did one date long distance? His car slowly drove along the tree-lined street, taking a huge chunk of her heart with him.

Chapter 24

The next morning, Tara hurried through her morning ritual with an eye on the clock. A sleepless night at least afforded her time to settle on exactly what she wanted to make for dessert. Now that she had Grant's help she could think clearly and make the necessary decisions. After a quick breakfast of a protein bar and cup of coffee, she pulled out the requisite cookbooks and made a list of the ingredients she'd need. As she stuffed the list into her purse, Roxie and Beth strode into the kitchen wearing matching khakis and dark green polos, ready for work.

"You're up early." Roxie snagged two mugs from the cupboard, handed one to Beth. "A right busy bee this morning."

"I didn't sleep well so thought I'd go to the store and get those boxes unpacked and the books in their proper places." Tara pushed to her feet, turned to snatch her purse from the shelf. "I'm meeting Grant for lunch and then shopping for what I need to make dessert for tomorrow."

"A second date?" Beth grinned as she poured coffee into her mug.

"Something like that." Tara shoved in her chair and slid her purse strap onto her shoulder. "I'll see you at the store."

No way would she say much about the whole first date. About the freaky fall, the terror in the dark, and then the puzzling test in Raven Hollow. Nor about the way they'd discovered a mutual attraction they couldn't deny no matter how hard she'd tried. She just wasn't sure if she could follow her heart down the path it wanted to go. Fraught with obstacles and potentially hurt feelings. She loved Grant. No doubt. Enough to not want to leave him with a broken heart when she couldn't move to the big city life he craved.

"Go ahead and open when you get there." Roxie cradled her mug in both hands as she peered at Tara. "I'll be right behind you. The holiday shopping season has arrived earlier than we'd predicted."

"Will do." Tara slipped on a light jacket over her forest polo and khakis, and fled the house.

She hurried down the quiet sidewalk along the tree-lined street she'd lived on all her life, glad of the mild temperature and light breeze. Past the huge oak standing on the corner where she'd fallen learning how to ride her bike. Past her childhood best friend's house, where they'd played with dolls and jumped rope. Past the local drug store where she'd embarrassed herself buying her first female products. She smelled rain in the air and hoped for a pretty day for their big dinner the next day. She turned onto Main, and the amount of traffic picked up on both the street and the sidewalks. Slipping her keys out of her purse, she selected one as she approached the door to the shop.

"Tara, got a minute?"

Startled, she addressed the source of the deep voice behind her when she halted and glanced over her shoulder. "Hey, Max. How are you?"

"Fine. I was hoping to grab breakfast from the Golden Owl, but I see you're not open yet."

"If you've got a minute, it won't take long to start the

coffee." Tara poked the key into the lock and swiftly opened the door.

Max consulted his watch. "That'll work. I don't have to be in my office for an hour."

She pushed open the door and hurried inside. Flipping on the lights, she waited for Max to step over the threshold and then closed the door. "Are you looking forward to tomorrow?"

She hustled to the coffee bar section, turning on lights as she went. First over the local authors display, then to illuminate the jewelry and stationery on consignment from local artisans. Two more switches to shed soft reading light throughout the stacks and shelves of books in the entire store. Finally, she flicked the switch for the lights over the coffee bar and pastry display case. A quick perusal of the area assured her all was ready for her to set out the bagels and buns on clean plates and start the coffee. She worked while Max took a seat at a café table in the front window nearby.

"Absolutely. Meredith and Paulette are both happy to have been invited. So am I and Zak, of course." He stretched his long legs out in front of him and crossed his ankles, leaning back in the chair while he observed her quick movements.

"Grant said he'd help me make dessert this afternoon." She glanced up from laying paper doilies onto the pedestal plates to look at the strikingly handsome older man. "I didn't know he knew his way around the kitchen."

"He's a renaissance man in many regards." Max chuckled and tapped a finger on the table. "Hey, since we're talking about Grant, maybe you can answer an off-the-wall question."

She stilled, holding the doily in front of her like a shield. She barely knew Grant. Not really. Her neck prickled with discomfort as she recalled snuggling with him. "I doubt that."

"Since you've been dating him…"

"Once."

Max inclined his head with a wry grin. "True, but I think you know him well enough to answer this question. Or I can just ask Zak?"

"Why don't you ask Grant?" Tara finished placing the doily on the last plate, pulled out the container of buns delivered the night before from a lady who baked them special for the store and started arranging them on the lacy paper. "He'd be your best source."

"I could, but since I'm here with you, let me ask you what you think." Max drummed his fingers once on the table and then laid his hand flat on the surface. "I've been working with a new environmental group moving into town. Do you think Grant would have any interest in relocating to Roseville for a job as a consultant?"

Grant move to town? He'd never given any indication he'd considered such a drastic change in his life. His career. She set the filled plate in the display case and wiped her hands on a paper towel. Delaying answering the question. Then she met Max's gaze.

"I don't think so. He loves the city life and the hustle and bustle too much to be happy in this sleepy town." Sad to say. Her heart couldn't take the highs and lows of the relationship, such as it was. Barely started and already causing pain. She heard the coffee brewer gurgle the last of the brew into the pot. Grateful for the distraction, she spun to fill a to-go cup with the hot liquid. Snapping a lid on, she turned to address him. "Even if he were to consider such a move."

"You may have a point. Oh well." Max pulled his feet under him and stood to cross to the counter. "I'll take one of those onion bagels, too."

"Did you want me to ask him when I see him?" Tara finished putting the bagel and a pack of cream cheese into a bag and sealed the top. Setting it beside the cup, she rang up the purchase. "He's stopping by later."

"No, there's no need. You're probably right." Max fished out the money to pay for his breakfast and handed it to Tara. "I'll ask around, see if anybody else might be interested."

She handed him the change. "I'll see you tomorrow, then."

With a wave of his hand, Max turned and strode quickly out of the store, the bell jangling into silence. She let her gaze drift around the cozy store. She loved her job, her home, her life. Most of all her sisters. She loved Grant, too. It was a shame she couldn't have both without sacrificing something or someone. What was she going to do?

Keep busy and focus on what she could control. She set to work, first putting out more of the pastries and cookies to go with the hot tea and coffee. As she wiped the counter, she envisioned the trajectory of a long-distance relationship with Grant. How they'd start out phoning frequently, texting perhaps. Then it would fall off to email exchanges every few days with a weekly call to chat and catch up. But time and distance would surely make their conversations fewer and less frequent. She couldn't give him her whole heart to have it shredded again.

The door opened to admit Roxie and Beth, bustling in with a rush of cool air accompanied by several customers trailing behind them. Not simply customers, but friends and neighbors she'd known all her life. She'd shared holidays and community events with them and in return, they supported the Golden Owl, not merely as paying patrons, but as people helping each other to survive in a crazy economy and uncertain times. Roseville was more than a small town. Roseville was her extended family. Simply put, she couldn't leave her family to strike out for parts unknown with a man she barely knew even though her heart begged her to consider making such a drastic change.

Beth took up her usual post at the coffee bar and began waiting on the line of people clamoring for buns and bagels to go with their morning brew. "I've got this, Tara."

"I'll be in the back." Tara wiped her hands on a paper towel and pitched it into the trash. "Yell if you need me."

Beth nodded but chatted with the next lady in line as Tara slipped out from behind the counter and ambled toward the work room. Late Monday afternoon, several large boxes of mysteries and romances had arrived from distributors. Big sellers during the holiday season. Her priority for the morning was to put them out on the shelves for sale. Tara saw Roxie across the store, winding through the round tables piled with books and other merchandise, finally stopping next to Tara.

Tara motioned toward the boxes visible through the open door to the work room. "I'll put out the new books before Grant comes at noon. Then we're going to be baking this afternoon."

"Sounds like a plan. Beth and I have our plan laid out for tomorrow's cooking fest." Roxie straightened a stack of bookmarks on the counter. "If you'll handle setting the table and such, and stay out of the kitchen, you'll live well and prosper."

"Thanks for the warning." Tara grinned as she headed toward the stock room. Best to keep her mind on her work and her family.

She only had a few hours before Grant arrived. When he did, she'd relish every minute in his company that day and the next. Try to stay focused on the time they'd share, the memories they'd make. Then she'd have to find a way to tell him goodbye.

Chapter Twenty-Five

$\mathcal{I}$f only time flowed as fast outside of the hollow as in it. Grant checked his watch again. Ten minutes had elapsed. Finally. He got out of his car and hurried to the Golden Owl. Pushing inside, the bell above the door announced his arrival. Tara smiled as she walked toward him, purse in hand. He returned the grin. She'd anticipated when he'd show up to take her to lunch.

"Hey, beautiful." He clasped her hand, glad to make contact after all the hours they'd spent apart. "Where do you want to eat?"

"Hey, handsome." She slipped the strap onto one shoulder as she considered his question. "We could grab something at the deli at Edna's while we pick up the ingredients we need. Take it home and eat?"

"Or I could take you to the Hideaway?" Grant had only eaten there once, and then it was a quick grab and go lunch with Zak. Sharing the intimate old jail cell turned into a dining room with Tara sounded like a better way to enjoy the noon meal. Surrounded by history in the company of the woman he planned to spend the rest of his life with.

"I'd rather carry a sandwich or something home so we

can start baking." Tara gripped the strap on her shoulder, fingers pale against the dark brown leather.

"So you've decided what we're making?" She seemed tense, but he chalked her reaction up to the whole baking concept. She had more ability than she wanted to admit, and he couldn't wait to help her discover that fact.

"Finally."

"Good." Grant pulled open the door, holding it for Tara to slip outside. "Let's go."

The bell jangled until the door thumped shut behind him. He caught up to Tara, helping her into his vehicle. Jogging around to the driver's side, he yanked the door open and practically leaped inside. Sitting next to her again, breathing in her perfume, seeing her lovely eyes and long, temptress locks, was heaven on earth. He'd not slept, tossing and turning, longing to snuggle with her again. To touch her, feel her silky skin beneath his hands.

He turned in his seat to look at her more closely. "So, what do you want to make?"

She snapped her seatbelt into place and then ticked off the items on one hand. "Pecan pie. Lemon meringue pie. And the best of all, angel food Waldorf cake."

"Impressive. I assume you've made the list of ingredients we need to buy?" He started the car, prepared to pull out to drive the few blocks to the grocery.

Tara tapped a forefinger to her purse. "All here."

They did the shopping in record time, selecting lunch from the deli's offerings. Back at the Golden house, he followed Tara up the sidewalk, carrying the several plastic bags of groceries hanging on both wrists. He dropped the sacks on the center island and rubbed the red marks on his skin.

Tara pulled out the bag of pecan halves and one of slivered almonds, dark brown sugar, confectioner's sugar, fresh lemons and strawberries, and a host of other items. He lifted the pecans and looked at Tara.

"What do you want to start with?"

"Lunch." She chuckled as she handed him a wrapped sandwich and bag of chips. "Tea?"

He nodded and carried his food to the table and sat. He glanced at Tara, sensing a restraint he'd not noticed previously. The sandwiches reminded him of their picnic, which in turn recalled how they'd ended up in Raven Hollow. Thinking about the sinkhole caused the horrible memories from his childhood to wash over him. Jeremy. He'd let him down, and although he'd attempted to assuage his guilt, he never had truly forgiven himself. He couldn't. He'd been the one at fault, and his friend had paid the price. He watched Tara pour sweet tea into two glasses and then carry them over to place them on the table. How had he found such a remarkable girl? His search for answers yielded much more than he'd ever imagined. But would she balk at tying her fortune to his wagon when she learned of his culpability in Jeremy's death?

She unwrapped her sandwich and then glanced up at him. Paused, her hands still on the wrapper. "What's wrong?"

"Nothing." Grant studied her, becoming aware she somehow could sense his feelings. Part of her gift. "Not really."

"You look upset. Tell me what's on your mind." She reached out with one hand, offering it to him like a lifeline. "Please?"

He wanted nothing more than to live out his days with this woman who waited for him to speak. She had the right to know his darkest secrets as a result. The right to know everything about him to help her make the choices she needed to make regarding her life. He placed his hand in hers and squeezed lightly.

"Remember I told you about my friend, Jeremy?"

"Your friend who died in the well?"

"Yes." He hesitated, wondering how she'd react to the

whole truth. "I didn't tell you everything about that day. In particular, my role in his death."

"Tell me what happened." She laid her other hand on top of their joined ones. Compassion simmered in her eyes, giving him the confidence he needed to spill out the story.

"I had heard about a dilapidated cabin in the hills near his home. I was burning with curiosity about the place, imagining all sorts of fantastic tales of how it fell into ruins. I convinced Jeremy to go with me. Not an easy task, but I can be pretty persuasive when I want something badly enough."

She lifted a brow and squeezed his hand. "I know. Go on."

"It was a whim, we just took off on our bikes and pedaled miles to the trailhead." His gaze turned inward, no longer seeing her. Reliving the day he lost his best friend due to his rash actions. "We didn't tell anyone where we were going or even take a canteen. I was stupid and too eager to seek out adventure."

"You were a boy." She squeezed his hand again to draw his attention. "That's what kids do."

"I was twelve. Old enough to have known better." He shrugged, pulling his hand back to clasp both together on the table. Uncomfortable with the recollection and recrimination he associated with the memory. "If I'd had a length of rope or even a belt I might have been able to save him."

"It sounds like it was a deep well." She peered at him for a short span. "Too deep for a belt to reach, surely."

"I could have tried."

"Grant, listen to me." She placed a hand on his clasped ones. "You were a kid, doing what kids do. Exploring, playing, taking risks you didn't fully understand. It's not your fault that he stepped on the well cover, nor that the wood gave way."

"It's my fault we were out there in the first place." He

raked a hand through his hair, gripping his nape until his neck hurt. "We shouldn't have gone so far from home."

"Maybe, but accidents happen. Did Jeremy's parents blame you?"

"No, they never said anything after that day."

"Then why do you blame yourself?" She squeezed his hand, her eyes steady on him. "Why not accept that bad things happen through no fault of your own."

"But..." He sighed as he pondered her words. "Maybe you're right. Maybe it was simply an accident, and nobody is to blame."

"That's what it seems like to me." She smiled at him, understanding and empathy in her eyes. "It's time for you to stop beating yourself up for something out of your control."

She made a good argument. He had been young and immature. But he had not led Jeremy to his death, only to the site of the house he wanted to explore. Nobody could have predicted how tragically events would unwind on that long ago day. Especially him as a young boy. He needed to move forward and stop letting the past haunt his present. His future beckoned with a bright light, fueled by the beautiful, caring woman sitting across from him.

"Thank you for understanding." He picked up his sandwich, ready to sample the mouth-watering meat and cheese. "So where do you want to start today?"

"I think the pecan pie is first." She lifted her sandwich and prepared to take a bite. "It won't take too long, right?"

He bit into his sandwich and then shook his head while he chewed and swallowed. "It'll keep well, too. So the pies and then the cake?"

"Sounds like a good plan." She nibbled her ham and cheese, her gaze on him. "I'm glad we compromised on the crusts."

"My mom always did, so I do." Some people might taste the difference between scratch and store-bought pie crust, but nobody had ever complained. He didn't see the need to spend the time on making pie crust dough and all that it entailed. "It saves frustration."

"I'm all about avoiding frustration." Tara took a small bite before laying her sandwich on the wrapper. "I'm ready to begin if you are."

"Not hungry?" He studied the remaining piece of his sandwich and then popped it into his mouth, chewing quickly. If his lady was anxious to begin, then he'd not keep her waiting. He wiped his hands on a paper napkin. "I'm all yours."

She smiled at him, a hint of caution behind her expression. "Very funny."

Grant pushed to his feet while Tara gathered the remains of their lunch. If she only knew how serious his flippant comment was to him. She threw away the trash and then moved to the island to open a cookbook laying on the clean surface. Flipping to a page marked with a length of ribbon, she leaned closer to study the contents. Even that proved sexy to him. Her cute butt swaying side to side as she hummed and read. A fingertip trailing down the page in a slow, tantalizing movement.

"It says to chop the pecans. How small, do you think?" She turned a wrinkled brow up at him. "Does size matter?"

He chuckled as he sidled over to peer over her shoulder at the recipe. "Better question is how large, don't you think?"

She rolled her eyes at him and shook her head. "Be serious."

Her scent enticed as he leaned closer, resting his hands on her shoulders. "I am."

He tugged her around to face him, inches separating them. He could not resist the temptation of her lips, slightly parted in surprise at his sudden move. Her eyes flicked between meeting his gaze and focusing on his mouth as he closed the distance between them. Sweet heaven. The taste of her when their lips met was better than the sugars on the counter. Sweeter than the taste of honeysuckle in the summer. He devoured her, exploring the depths of her mouth, letting his eyes drift shut, so he only knew her and nothing outside of the delectable woman in his arms.

Minutes passed, and then he slowly broke away, dragging in a long breath as she opened her eyes. Unfocused. As if she'd experienced the mind-blowing kiss as much as he had. He pressed a kiss to her lips and then laid a finger on them, watching her gaze clear and a smile light her eyes. Man, did he have it bad for her.

"I suppose you're right." Her lips moved beneath his finger until he lifted it away. "Size does matter."

He huffed and then kissed her again. He simply couldn't help himself. "Let me show you how to cut them to the right size."

She spun away, to face the counter and the set of knives in a wooden block in the center. "Choose your weapon."

He reached around her and slid one out of its home, hefted the well-balanced blade. Someone, probably her mother, had fine taste in kitchen utensils and tools for cooking. His first assessment of the functionality of the space proved even more correct. Everything about the house fit his taste and his expectations. Especially the woman standing in front of him.

Over the next couple of hours they worked together. He kept her near and within his embrace as much as possible as they moved from task to task. He made a point of brushing her arm in passing. Of lightly resting a hand on her shoulder, or planting a kiss on the side of her neck as he eased around her to retrieve the vanilla or sift the flour. Tug on her ponytail when he moved to locate eggs in the fridge. He wanted her to know how much she meant to him. How much he desired to be with her even if he did have to return to his job. He knew she'd never leave her hometown unless forced to. He'd not be the reason. He loved her too much to ask her to make such a sacrifice.

Still, the thought of leaving evoked a sense of despair in his soul. Sure, he'd floated the idea of staying in Roseville, but how could he without a job? He couldn't support a wife and eventually a family without a source of income. Which currently existed in another state. And left him in a state of anxiety unlike any he'd ever endured. For the present, he'd touch and taste her much like a fine wine or an elegant dessert. Savor every moment with her. Memorize her every move, inflection, and expression to carry with him. Until he found a way to return to her side for good.

Tara wiped her hands on a towel and grinned at him. "That finishes the pies, and the cake is baked and ready for the final construction."

"Are we building something?" Grant loved her quirky little smile at his question.

"You could say that. We need to slice off the top of the cake, then cut out a tunnel in the bottom and pull out the center part of the cake." She motioned with her hands to show him what she meant. "Then we fill the tunnel with whipped cream, sliced strawberries, and slivered almonds."

"Yum." She was so cute when she wrinkled her brow in thought. "Then what?"

"Put the top on and smother the whole thing in more whipped cream." She pointed to a second box of strawberries. "Some of those get spaced on top as decoration."

"Double yum." He gazed at his woman, drinking in her features and enjoying her animated motions with her hands. "What happens to the cake you pull out?"

She wiggled her brows with a grin aimed his direction. "That's the best part. You get to eat it."

"I'm in." He propped his hands on her shoulders and gently spun her around to meet his gaze. "You're an amazing woman, Tara."

She canted her head, a question in her eyes. "I see I've got you fooled."

"No, I see you." He squeezed her upper arms, searching her eyes for several moments. "I love you."

That hint of wariness appeared again in her eyes as she regarded him for a heartbeat. "I love you, too."

"We'll work it out, now that we've found our way back to civilization."

She raised her brows a fraction of an inch, pursing her lips for a moment. "I hope so but it may be more difficult than we think."

She didn't bother to deny she'd been concerned about the same thing. Remarkable woman, indeed. Almost as if she could read his mind. But that wasn't possible. Was it?

"Tara, don't give up on me. On us." She had to believe in him, trust him, as much as he did her. "We'll always be together. I promise."

She nodded slowly as she eased a step away, breaking contact with him as her expression sobered. "For now, let's enjoy the holiday and worry about the future next week."

"When I leave?" The mere idea of not being able to touch Tara festered deep in his chest. He'd figure out a means of being with her. He must.

"When you leave the hard part begins."

"For both of us." Grant closed the small space between them, placing a finger under her chin to raise her gaze to meet his. "You know that. Don't you?"

She inhaled sharply and nodded once. "Right. Let's get this done before my sisters come home."

"Very well. What do you need me to do?" He would honor her wishes for now. He had no other good choice but to follow the plan.

Soon, he'd devise a strategy for how to keep his promise. To her and to himself.

Chapter Twenty-Six

*R*ain lashed the dining room windows, pelting hail against the sashes. Tara glared at the water cascading down the outside of the pane. She'd hoped for a sunny Thanksgiving, but nature had other plans. She searched through the dresser drawer reserved for tablecloths until she found the dark orange one imprinted with pale gold and burgundy leaves as well as the memory of past family dinners when her mother had acted as hostess. She lifted the lightweight, soft fabric and then pushed the drawer closed with her hip as the sound of her sisters fussing echoed through the short hallway. Good thing the desserts were already done, so she didn't need to venture into that tiny kitchen with too many cooks.

With eight expected for dinner, she'd added a couple of leaves to the table. She shook out the cloth before draping it over the wood surface, smoothing out wrinkles with her palms. So many memories clamored for her attention, but she merely let them swirl into the background as she retrieved the centerpiece from the sideboard. Simple yet appropriate. She set the large, flat glass bowl with a lone gold pillar candle nestled among whole walnuts, pecans, and hazelnuts. A reminder of the lessons she learned in Raven

Hollow. She rotated the bowl slightly to the left, then made a few adjustments to the arrangement of the nuts. Stepping away from the table, she smiled.

The doorbell rang, startling her. Nobody came to the front door of the house. Practically the entire town felt welcome at the back door. The townsfolk treated the three sisters like their own kin and had as long as Tara could recall. So who had rung the bell at the front? She hurried into the hall.

"I'll get it!" She paused for a response but heard only bickering from the kitchen.

She shook her head as she strode to unlock the door and pull it open. A small crowd huddled on the covered porch, shivering in an assortment of rain gear. Her cousins, Meredith and Paulette, and their husbands, Max and Zak, respectively. And of course Paulette's newborn son. Standing one step behind the others, not quite covered by the porch roof, Grant waited with one hand on the white column supporting the tin overhead. Her heart swelled at the sight of him, the memory of his kisses as they worked together. Heat flared on her cheeks when she remembered the others impatiently waiting to be let into the warm house.

"Goodness, get that baby out of the cold." Tara stepped back to urge everyone inside.

"It's awful out there." Paulette stepped across the threshold; little Pat bundled so he was barely visible in his infant carrier. Zak followed right behind them carrying a bulging tote bag.

Meredith shivered as she passed through the doorway, then Max came in close behind her. "I can't believe it turned so cold so fast."

"I know. I'm sorry you had to face the deluge. Let me have your coats." She held out her hands, waiting for them to shed their outer garments, aware of Grant's every step as he trailed in after the others. "Why did you come to the front door?"

Paulette set the carrier down and wriggled out of her dripping coat. Zak shrugged out of his slicker, grabbed his wife's, and then offered them to Tara. "It's a shorter distance from the street out front than to the back door."

"Right. Come on in. Beth and Roxie are stirring up trouble, or rather dinner." Tara took the others' coats and hung them on a free-standing coat rack tucked in a nook along the hallway.

Grant came up behind her, reached around to hang his jacket on the last hook. "I've missed you."

She spun around, lifting her gaze to meet his smile. "It's only been half a day."

"I know. Too long." He kissed her, light and easy with the promise of much more to come.

She sighed with a smile on her lips. When he left, she'd only have these memories to keep him close. "Tempting me again, huh?"

"Always." Grant chuckled, the sound reverberating in Tara's chest pressed up to his.

"Behave." Tara pushed him away from her, giving her space to breathe and chance for her pulse to calm.

"If you insist." He winked at her.

"I do." How else could she maintain her equilibrium in front of her family? Knowing the hours ticked away too fast for her peace of mind.

"Should we come back later?" Max asked with a smirk.

"Ignore Grant. Follow me." Tara, cheeks flaming, led the way to the dining room. The urgent murmur from the kitchen drifted down the hall, punctuated by bursts of laughter. She paused at the door to the dining room. "I was just setting the table."

"Staying out of the way?" Paulette held the carrier with both hands, little Pat's eyes blinking awake as he yawned.

"Look at how adorable he is." Tara pulled the pale yellow blanket away from the one-month-old baby's face so she could see his cute nose and tiny mouth. A hat covered his head so she couldn't see more than his round face. "He's growing so."

"He eats enough, let me tell ya." Paulette beamed with contentment and motherly pride. A good look for her.

Zak hefted the tote. "We brought wine. Where shall I put it?"

Tara straightened to regard Grant's handsome brother. He'd been part of Roseville for little more than a month, but already had found employment as a chemical engineer for a local defense contractor. Like Grant, he'd only planned to visit for a spell, but Paulette had changed his mind. If only Tara could change Grant's. A depressing thought when she hadn't the heart to make him forego living in the kind of environment most pleasing to him. Love shouldn't require such a huge sacrifice. Should it? Could she sacrifice living in Roseville to be with Grant in the city? Give up the comforting surroundings, memories, and people she'd depended on her entire life? At the moment, watching Grant meld with her family seamlessly, she thought maybe she could. Witnessing him laughing and teasing his brother, her heart swelled with love for the man.

"I'd say the kitchen, but you really don't want to go there." Tara pointed to the sideboard with a wave of her hand. "The sideboard works."

"Want some help with the table?" Meredith scanned the room and then winked at Tara. "Busy hands are better than idle ones, our grandmother always said."

"Us men folk will take Pat and get out of the way in the

living room." Max chuckled and glanced around the room. "Unless you need us to do something?"

"Nope. Shoo." Tara grinned at the guys as they made good on Max's plan.

"I'm happy to help, too." Paulette rubbed her palms together. "What do you need me to do?"

Tara rattled off a short list of tasks and the three women set to work. Before many minutes had passed, the table was ready for the roasted turkey and all its trimmings. Tara surveyed the results and then ushered her cousins into the living room.

"Something smells good enough to eat." Zak greeted her with a smile and a lift of the cocktail in his hand.

"I'm glad you've made yourselves at home." Tara glanced to Grant, who shrugged. He'd become familiar with the lay of the house during his visits over the past few days. "Where's mine?"

Grant rose from where he'd been sitting by the gas fireplace, converted years before from the wood burning type. The heat from the flickering flames removed the chill in the air created by the cold rain falling outside. He strode over to the rolling cart serving as the bar, several bottles of colorful liquor and an array of glasses and tools gleamed in the lamplight. Tara had filled the ice bucket before starting on the dining room, anticipating this very scene. She knew the men in her life.

"The bar is open. What will you have?" Grant swiped a hand over the display.

The ladies placed their orders, and Grant set to work filling them in record time. Just as he handed the last glass to Tara, footsteps sounded in the hall. She looked to the doorway as Beth and Roxie sashayed into the room. Tara expected to see dishevelment in their attire, but both were neat and tidy. After all the ruckus, they appeared none the worse. Even excited and energized.

Roxie surveyed the group with a content grin. "Grant, if you'd be so kind, would you fix me a Manhattan? Extra cherry syrup?"

Grant inclined his head to her. "Beth?"

"Same, please." Beth sank onto a vacant seat on the sofa beside Meredith. "After we've enjoyed our drinks, it will be time to eat."

Tara watched Grant pour bourbon and sweet vermouth into the shaker. He added ice, then bitters. Topped it off with some cherry syrup from the jar of maraschino cherries. He put the lid on and shook the mixture several times, the muscles on his upper arms flexing in the most tantalizing way. She blinked, focusing then on the smile he aimed her way. She lifted one brow in answer to his knowing look, then turned to listen to the conversation flowing around the silent exchange. Pretended to no longer be aware of his actions as he poured the concoction into rock glasses and dropped a cherry into each with strong fingers that she knew from experience felt wonderful wrapped around her. A warm buzz filled her chest at the memory. Time to think about anything else if she had any hope of maintaining her composure.

"Did you need someone to carve?" Max sipped his martini, a large green olive rolling slowly around as he tilted and then straightened the wide-mouthed glass.

Roxie accepted a glass with its dark red blend of liquor. "All taken care of. I'm letting the gravy simmer a while."

"Not too long, I hope." Grant moved to stand beside the wing back chair where Tara sat. He held a martini glass in one hand, the clear liquor revealing a lone olive in the bottom. "I'm starving."

"Again?" Tara aimed an innocent smile up at him, batting her lashes at his surprised expression. "You're always eating something."

He chuckled and shrugged, sipped. "I'm a growing boy."

Tara laughed at the absurdity of his claim. "Right. And I'm Betty Crocker."

The banter continued in the same vein until Roxie finished her cocktail. Then she cleared her throat and stood, aiming a smile at each person as she addressed them. "Turkey time. Beth, Tara, will you put the side dishes on the table, please? Max, since you asked about the turkey, would you bring the platter in? Meredith and Paulette can head to the table. Zak and Grant can pour the wine. I'll get the gravy. We'll be set."

"Yes, ma'am." Zak helped Paulette to her feet, and handed the infant carrier to her. "Sweetheart, take Pat and make yourselves comfortable. The rest of us have our marching orders."

Grant offered Tara a hand to help her stand, pulling her close for a quick kiss. "If you need help with anything, anything at all, let me know."

She squeezed his hand and then released it. "We've got this." She gave him a little push with one hand. "Go on. We'll eat shortly so you won't be starving any longer."

True to her promise, amidst jostling and joking, the food was on the table, the wine was in the glasses, and everybody had taken their places around the harvest bounty. Tara mentally ticked off the menu to make sure they hadn't forgotten anything. Sliced turkey, both dark and white meat, took pride of place on a large platter before Roxie. The gravy boat sat nearby. Bowls of green bean casserole, glazed cinnamon carrots, corn, mashed and candied sweet potatoes sent wisps of steam and their aromas mingling in the air. Beth's signature cranberry sauce glimmered in its glass bowl as it was passed eagerly from hand to hand.

Pat, on the floor in his carrier, started to cry beside Paulette. She reached down to soothe him with a quiet word and gentle rocking of his carrier. After he settled into a contented silence, she straightened in her chair.

As if on a silent signal, Roxie lifted her wine glass. "Before we eat, I'd like to propose a toast."

"Another delay?" Grant picked up his glass.

"A short toast." Roxie grinned at him and then let her gaze light on each person at the table. "To our family and all those we love on this day of thanksgiving."

Tara clinked glasses with Grant, sitting to her left, and then with Meredith on her right. As everyone took a sip from their glasses, she realized something she'd never considered before. An idea she mulled as she sipped her wine, thinking of each person surrounding her in the small dining room.

"Can we eat now?" Grant asked, reaching for the casserole nearest him.

Roxie nodded and reached for the meat fork on the turkey platter. "If you'll pass your plates, I'll dish up the turkey. The platter's too heavy to pass."

"I hope I didn't put too much pepper in the beans." Beth tightened her mouth, worry evident in her eyes.

"Is there such a thing?" Zak spooned dollops of mashed potatoes onto his plate. "I like spicy."

The conversation cemented the burgeoning thought. Tara poured gravy onto her turkey and mashed potatoes, then passed the dish to Meredith. "I just realized something."

Grant glanced at her, an inquiring expression on his face. "What's that?"

"I always thought Thanksgiving was about the food. You know, the bounty of the harvest and all that." She looked from one to the other of the people around her. "But it's not. Not really. It's about coming together to be grateful for the family and friends we have in our lives."

If the lessons of the hollow had done nothing else, they made her aware of the importance of the people she loved. She turned to Grant, laid a hand on his arm and squeezed.

He nodded slowly, a small smile lifting his lips as he regarded her.

"Well said." Roxie smiled at her. "Even if the food flops, as long as we have someone who cares about and for us, we have much to be thankful for."

"The gathering together to share a special day, or even an ordinary day. The people we call family and friends are the reason for being thankful." Tara returned the smile to her sister, understanding relaxing her tension about whether she could pass her sister's test. She had succeeded by not relying solely on her own skills. Recognizing when she needed help and being willing to open her heart and mind to others and their abilities.

"Speaking of people in our lives." Max added cranberry sauce to his plate, set the bowl down, and then looked at Grant. "I was contacted by a first response environmental organization opening a new office here in town."

"Why are you looking at me when you say that?" Grant speared a bite of turkey, dredged it through his mashed potatoes, and then put it in his mouth. "I'm not a first responder."

"I didn't say you are." Max speared a bit of turkey and held it aloft. "I think you can help me, though."

Grant sipped his wine and set the glass on the table. "With what?"

"They're looking for an environmental consultant. I don't know anyone, since from what Tara said you're happy with your job." Max took a sip of wine, swallowed as he looked at Grant.

Grant cut a look at Tara and then addressed Max again. "What does she have to do with my job? I'm confused."

Tara laid a hand on his arm. "He asked me if I thought you'd be interested in living in Roseville. I told him I didn't think so."

"I—" He hadn't seriously considered moving to the

town, because without any means to support himself, let alone anyone else, such a move wasn't feasible. But… "Why don't you think I'd want to live here?"

Tara shrugged and looked at her plate. Afraid to address her fear that he would in fact leave and never return because the town held nothing of interest. "There's nothing to do here compared to all the culture and activities in the big city, what you referred to as civilization. I didn't think you'd be content."

Grant shifted beside her so he could snare her chin with his fingers and make her lift her head to look at him. "You're here. That's the only reason I need to want to live here."

She blinked at him slowly as she inspected his eyes looking for any hint of insincerity or subterfuge. Saw only honest, urgent hope. "Really?"

"Yes." Grant leaned over to plant a kiss on her mouth, then with a wink turned to address Max. "What is this company looking for?"

"They're looking for a professional geologist," Max said, breaking a crescent roll in two. "I thought I'd ask you if you were interested or could recommend a colleague."

Grant dropped his fork onto his plate, the ring of china echoing in the still room. "A geologist?"

Max raised both brows, a wicked smile aimed at Grant. "Yeah. Do you know anyone who might consider moving to a small town like this?"

"I think I most definitely do." Grant grinned and nodded. "Me."

"Really? That's great. You're more than qualified for the position, which is why I thought of you." Max looked pleased. "I'll give you their contact information after dinner. I'm positive they'd welcome you with open arms."

"Thanks. That means…" Grant turned toward Tara, and took her hand in his.

Her pulse kicked up several notches when she noticed a gleam in his eyes as he pushed back from the table. Tugged on her hand to draw her to stand beside him. A hush fell over the table at the strange tableau. Six pairs of eyes aimed at her and Grant where they stood beside the table, facing each other.

"Tara, I know we've only known each other a short time. But I also know I cannot live without you. In fact, I don't want to live without you in my life every single day."

Tears filled her eyes, but she held them in. Waited to hear what she hoped to hear with every filament in her body.

"Tara Golden, if you'll marry me, I promise to stay by your side, live here in Roseville where you want to be for the rest of your life. I'll do all in my power to ensure your happiness, contentment, and safety as long as I draw breath. Will you marry me, Tara?"

"Oh, Grant..." Tears leaked from her eyes, and she smiled through them. "I want nothing more than to be your wife. Yes, of course, I'll marry you."

He let out a whoop as he scooped her into his arms and spun around, laughing. Behind them, the table erupted in clapping and laughter. Tara felt a little dizzy from all the commotion and spinning, but happy in so many ways. After he set her on her feet, she held onto his arm until the room stopped spinning. Then she smiled at him.

"Grant, there's only one thing you have to promise me." She studied him, joy and a bit of devilment in her heart.

"Anything." He slowly shook his head side to side as he smiled at her, holding both her hands in his. "You only have to ask, and I'll give you whatever you want."

She wiped the smile from her face as she regarded him as seriously as she could. "The next time we go hiking..."

"If we go hiking?"

"When we go hiking." She grinned at him. She couldn't

help it. The perplexed look he aimed her way proved too funny to ignore. "Let's go on a very different trail than last time. Okay?"

He burst out laughing and then planted a long kiss on her lips. Pulling away, he grinned at her. "That's a promise I'm happy to make."

The End

Thanks so much for reading *The Touchstone of Raven Hollow* I hope you enjoyed Tara and Grant's story. Beth meets a sexy and daring airman, Mitch Sawyer, who entices her into danger in *Veiled Visions of Love*, the fourth book in the series.

To find out about new releases and upcoming appearances, please sign up for my newsletter via my website at www.bettybolte.com. I send out a monthly newsletter with book news to share with my readers, upcoming events and signings, and even a few favorite recipes, puzzles, and other doings!

I'd love to hear from you! Feel free to send me an email at betty@bettybolte.com, find me on Facebook at AuthorBettyBolte, follow me on BookBub, or connect with me on Twitter @BettyBolte.

You can always find an updated list of the titles in this series, as well as all of my other books on my website, at www.bettybolte.com/books/.

Thanks again for reading!

9 780998 162553